Praise for *Racing the Devil*

"A smart story, well-constructed and well told." –*Booklist*

"Carve out a chunk of free time to read this novel, because you won't be able to put it down until you reach the end of this tale." –*Suspense Magazine*

"*Racing the Devil* is a top-quality read from a promising writer." –*Mystery Scene Magazine*

"*Racing the Devil* is one of the best detective mysteries I've read in a long time...Exceptionally good writing, terrific new protagonist, colorful setting." –*Wayne Dundee, author of the Drifter Detective series and the Bounty Hunter series*

Praise for *A Cup Full of Midnight*

"If there's anything Terrell can't do, you wouldn't know it from reading *A Cup Full of Midnight*. This is a riveting, deeply felt novel with a terrific mystery at its core." –*Timothy Hallinan, author of the critically acclaimed Poke Rafferty Bangkok thrillers*

"If Taylor Jackson ever needed a private investigator, she would call Jared McKean." –*J. T. Ellison, New York Times bestselling author of the Taylor Jackson and Samantha Owen series*

"The perfect combination of noir and human hope." –*Sheila Deeth, Café Libre, author of* Divide by Zero

"The best thing about this book is the main character, Jared

McKean, who is one of the best protagonists that I have ever read about." –*Michael A. Wood, The Critical Critic*

Praise for *River of Glass*

"Pleasingly spiky prose which positively bristles with the darker side of wit. This is strongly recommended." –*San Francisco Book Review, 5 Stars*

"The same deft characterization we've seen in Terrell's other novels...Terrell plays fair so the reader can always see the logic in the twist, but in RIVER, the twist is so unexpected, it left this reader breathless." –*Nancy Sartor, award-winning author of* Bones Along the Hill *and* Blessed Curse

"Terrell has a knack for telling gritty stories that look at real-life possibilities, but the best part of everything I've read so far is her ability to create characters that come alive. –*Jerri Lynn Ledford, author of* Biloxi Blue *and* Biloxi Sunrise

Praise for *A Taste of Blood and Ashes*

"A vision of beauty and pain that leaves behind a taste of the truth in between." –*Sheila's Reviews*

"Another entertaining entry in a consistently solid series." –*Booklist*

"Excellent characters, a great plot and a marvelous attention to detail make this one hard to put down." –*Brett Bias, Amazon reviewer*

"[Jaden Terrell's] Jared McKean series is one of my favorites. Her writing is so beautiful, it touches my emotions on every level. . . . If you want beautiful writing, tight plotting, an edge-of-your-seat story, this book is for you." *–Lover of Books, Amazon reviewer*

TROUBLE MOST FAIRE

Familiar Legacy #11

JADEN TERRELL

Jaden Terrell

KaliOka Press

Cover design by Cissy Hartley

This book is dedicated to David Terrell. Here's to many more adventures together. Love you, baby brother.

Mappe of the Faire

SHERWOOD REN FAIRE BASE MAP

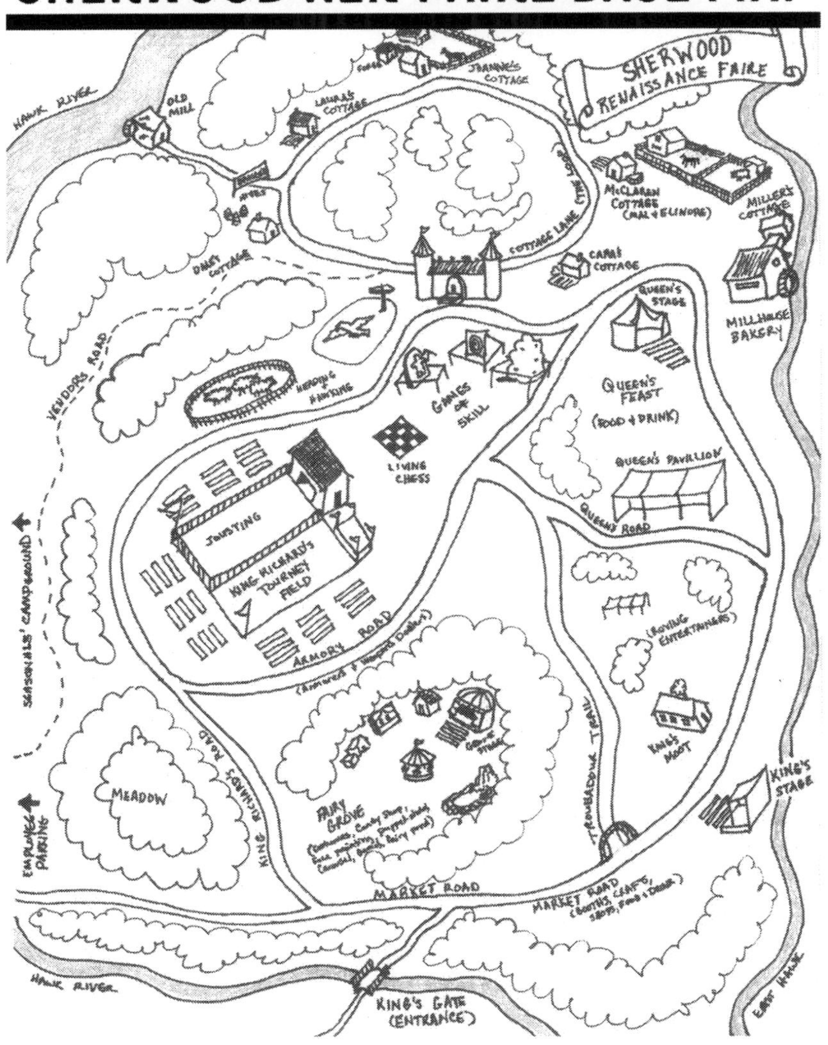

CHAPTER ONE

Trouble, the world-famous black cat detective, creeps forward on stealthy paws as his arch-enemy, an international spy cleverly disguised as a gray squirrel, nibbles on a pine nut, oblivious to its peril.

All right, peril might be overstating it a bit. I'm far too cultured a gentleman to actually commit rodenticide. Nonetheless, we crime-solving felines must keep our reflexes honed.

Although I miss my biped, Tammy Lynn, I must admit I'm enjoying my stay at the Sherwood Renaissance Faire. Tammy's friend Laura is providing me lodgings while Tammy spends a month in Europe on a rare book tour. I can hardly wait to hear about the literary treasures she'll encounter on her travels. In the meantime, Laura prepares a gourmet dish for me each evening, and while I dine on crisp sea bass or succulent shrimp, we watch DVDs of Benedict Cumberbatch playing Sherlock on her wide-screen telly. Tammy must have told her Sherlock is one of my role models, and that Cumberbatch's version is my favorite. My father, who is also a famous detective, is a role model as well, but he's more of a Sam Spade type.

Occasionally, Laura devotes an evening to what she calls my education in geek culture, and we watch programs like Star Trek, Star Wars, *and* Doctor Who.

During the day I have the run of the faire grounds, while the year-round employees—otherwise known as the Rennies (or collectively, the Troupe)—prepare for next month's opening. Laura is a Rennie. The Seasonals will begin arriving soon, and in the meantime, I bask in the mid-March Tennessee sun, explore the grounds, and practice my stalking skills by counting coup on local fauna like this squirrel.

I'm almost close enough to tap his tail when a woman's voice comes from around a bend in the trail, uttering a quiet, singsong litany of invectives. I recognize them from a documentary I once saw about the Middle Ages in a segment called "Medieval Curses and Insults." Among my many areas of expertise, I am, if I may say so myself, a well-versed Anglophile. Thus, my rather posh British accent, fashioned after Cumberbatch's, is more refined than the speech of the other cats in my Alabama hometown of Wetumpka.

"Pediculous ninnyhammer," she says. And, "Puke-stocking, caddis-gartered, addle-pated mumblecrest!"

The squirrel tenses. As he glances toward the voice, he catches sight of me and leaps sideways with a little squeak. I fix my gaze on him, and he scampers up the nearest tree. Silly little git. I smile to myself, imagining the tales he'll tell the other squirrels about his narrow escape from the jaws—and claws—of death.

I turn my attention to the path, and a moment later a pretty young woman covered in dust trudges into view, holding what appears to be a hawk carrier in one hand and a small leather purse in the other. Beneath the scents of lavender soap and sweat, I can clearly smell the aroma of a raptor. It has a wild tang one never smells in domestic poultry.

"Zooterkins! Jobberknowl! Nobthatcher!"

The woman is on the small side for a human, and the carrier is, if my memory of avian taxonomy serves me, of a size most likely to contain a kestrel. Kestrels are the smallest of the North American raptors, a size well-suited to this diminutive female.

Interesting.

The woman is wearing khaki trousers and a T-shirt embroidered with an archery logo captioned, "Silent but Deadly." Her hair, the golden-brown of a perfectly-toasted buttermilk biscuit, is limp with sweat. She blows her fringe out of her eyes and says, "Codswallop. It's hot out here."

She stops short, looks at me, and flashes an exhausted smile. "Well. Hello, handsome."

I like her already. Clearly, this is a woman of impeccable taste.

THE BLACK CAT rolled onto his back across the trail and batted at a dust mote. He looked sleek and well fed, his eyes clear and greenish-gold in the dappled sunlight. Robbi set the kestrel carrier down and rubbed her aching arms. "Are you lost, big fella?"

The cat cocked his head and graced her with an indignant meow. No, not lost. He looked too well cared for to be a stray.

She pushed a damp strand of hair away from her face and sighed. This wasn't how she'd planned to make her grand entrance, footsore and covered in trail dust. But her car, the miniature SUV she jokingly called "Old Reliable" because it was anything but, had sputtered to a halt six miles back.

She set down the carrier, then reached into her back pocket and pulled out the hand-scrawled map her best friend Laura had sent. Yes, there was the bend she'd just come around, and just beyond the cat was the footbridge spanning a narrow section of the river. Not far now. Then she could freshen up a bit at Laura's cottage and gulp down a gallon of ice water before calling for a tow and meeting the rest of the Troupe.

She'd just folded the map and stuffed it back into her pocket when a shriek cut through the stillness, followed by the violent rustling of the underbrush on the far side of the bridge, another long squeal, and a stream of curses more colorful than her own. A small potbellied pig hurtled out of the trees, pursued by the tallest, most muscular woman Robbi had ever seen.

"You little...! Why, I'll..." The woman gasped, narrowly missing the pig with a blow from her hand axe. "I warned you, Tuck, you little glutton! You'll be bacon by bedtime!"

Robbi stepped onto the footbridge. The pig shot past her and she spread her arms wide to block the axe-wielder, who skidded to a stop in the middle of the bridge and glowered past her at the pig. The pig slowed to a trot and then dropped, panting, into the dust beside the cat.

Robbi swallowed. The woman looked even bigger at this distance, thick and mannish, with bulging biceps, callused hands, and an angry red face. In her tunic and trousers, blacksmith's apron, and leather boots, she might have stepped out of a medieval painting. She glared at Robbi and growled, "Step aside, princess."

Princess? Robbi suppressed a laugh. "I don't think so."

"Little early for a Seasonal, aren't you? Any rate, this is not your business."

"What's your problem with the pig? Tuck, you said?"

"Third time this week he's raided the horse feed, the thievin' little scoundrel. Now let me by before I..." The woman shook the axe, stuck out her chin. "Don't make me pitch you in the river."

Robbi's shoulders tensed. Was she really going to get into a brawl on her first day here? And with a giantess, no less?

She blew out a slow breath and sank into a defensive stance, like her Tai Chi *sifu* had taught her. "Are you sure you wouldn't rather just grab a couple of ales and talk it out?"

The woman's eyes narrowed. She glared at the pig again, then at Robbi. Flinging the axe away, she charged.

Robbi wasn't about to abandon the pig. But the woman had a good ten inches and at least fifty pounds on her, so a grappling defense was impossible. Instead, she'd have to use her attacker's size and weight for leverage. Borrow her force, as her instructor would say. Robbi took a step toward the railing, then launched herself forward to meet the charge. As she ducked into the woman's punch, her left hand clasped and pulled the attacker's wrist, while her right palm pushed against the woman's opposite shoulder. Momentum lifted the giantess off her feet and spun her over the railing.

Ha!

Time seemed to slow, and for a moment Robbi saw it like a snapshot—the woman's flailing arms, her widening eyes, her broad mouth open in a startled "o." Robbi heard a bark from the far side of the bridge, then caught a flash of movement as a red border collie and a man in a kilt ran toward her from the trees where she'd first seen the pig.

Then time snapped back into place. As the giantess fell, her huge hand clamped over Robbi's arm and yanked her off her feet. The wooden rails flashed past, then spinning trees and patches of sky.

Robbi had just time enough to fill her lungs before the icy water closed over her.

Codswallop!

MAL MCCLAREN CLATTERED onto the bridge and looked over the railing into the water below, which churned with flailing fists and protruding elbows. He couldn't tell who was winning. The newcomer's move had been impressive, but the larger woman had the advantage now.

"Joanne!" he shouted. "Stop!"

With Miss Scarlett at his heels, Mal bolted across the bridge and ran past Tuck and the black cat, Trouble, who sat watching the spectacle with interest. Tuck seemed all of a piece, thank goodness. When the pig's squeals had trailed off, Mal had imagined the worst and prayed for the best. He'd known Joanne for four years, but he'd never been certain how much of her hot temper was bluster.

Mal bounded down the bank and splashed into the river, gasping as the icy water soaked through his leather boots and woolen socks. Despite the long shirt tucked into his waistband, he felt a twinge of embarrassment as the current lifted his kilt. Then the two women came up, sputtering and coughing. Joanne stood up in water to her waist, blacksmith's apron dripping, water streaming from her short-cropped hair. The smaller woman clambered to her feet.

"For the love of..." Mal splashed toward them, his kilt swirling around his thighs. The women turned to look at him, then back at each other. Joanne's mouth twitched. Her shoulders shook. The stranger tried and failed to suppress a giggle.

Then they were both laughing, and Mal was laughing with them, half with relief and half from self-consciousness.

He held out a hand to Joanne and hauled her back into the shallows. As she climbed onto the bank, he turned back to the smaller woman.

Still smiling, she pushed her hair from her eyes. They were spectacular eyes, big and brown, filled with a mischievous twinkle and framed with long, thick lashes. She looked intelligent, he thought. And not too hard on the eyes, either, even if she did resemble a half-drowned dormouse.

Exactly the kind of woman he went for.

Exactly the kind of woman who meant trouble.

His smile faltering, he held out his hand again, but she didn't take it. Instead, eyes widening, she looked past his shoulder toward the bridge.

"What's that?" she said. And then, "Oh. Oh, no."

IT WAS the billow of white beneath the bridge that had caught Robbi's eye. A plastic garbage bag, she thought. Then, no, too heavy, too voluminous. More like a bedsheet.

Or a woman's skirt.

Funny how life could turn in an instant. One minute she was admiring the dimple in a blue-eyed Scotsman's cheek, and the next she was splashing toward something her heart refused to admit was anything more than flotsam.

She could see it more clearly now, the textured cloth, the pale hand bobbing on the ripples, the long hair splayed across the surface of the river, dark with water but an unmistakably familiar shade of red. The face was turned away, but Robbi knew. Then a small swell rocked the body, and the head tipped upward to reveal bloodless cheeks and sightless eyes.

Robbi lurched forward, crying out. A strong arm wrapped around her waist and pulled her back. "No, lass, no."

Some part of her mind was aware of his words as he half-tugged, half-carried her to shore, but she could make no sense of them. *Wait on the bank...Too late to help her...Call the police...* At the edge of her vision, she saw a sleek black shape slink down the bank. The cat.

The Scotsman turned her toward him, and she buried her face in his shirt. It smelled of river water and clean linen. A comforting hint of male musk.

"What is it?" said a gruff female voice. The giantess. "What's wrong?"

Robbi found her voice. "Under the bridge," she said, a hitch in her words. "It's Laura."

CHAPTER TWO

I have never lost a human in my charge. Oh, humans have been killed, but never my *human, never a human Tammy has asked me to watch over. It's a dreadful feeling, made worse by the thought that if I'd been with Laura instead of prowling the grounds and trifling with the squirrel, she might be alive.*

Could some stranger have accosted her? Or could it have been one of the Rennies? I knew there was tension between Laura and various members of the Troupe, but I'd seen nothing severe enough to lead to her death. Not in the short time I've been here.

But I am making an assumption, which a detective should always avoid. Perhaps this was simply a freakish accident; perhaps this perfectly healthy young woman, dressed more for a ball than for a walk in the woods, stumbled and hit her head, or fainted from a tightly-fitting corset. Not that she typically wore one, but in that dress, I'm sure she would have. It's a costume piece, not everyday wear, and she would have wanted the fit to be authentic. At any rate, back when they were common, tight corsets were a frequent cause of vapours in women.

It seems plausible, barely. But I know better. I can feel it in my whiskers.

Someone did this to her, and I intend to find out who.

EVEN AS SHE clambered up the bank, Robbi was fishing for her cell phone. Dead. Expired. Shuffled off this mortal coil and gone to meet its maker, as they said in Monty Python's iconic parrot sketch. She and Laura must have watched that sketch a thousand times, each time shrieking, "*Pining for the fjords?!*" and collapsing into giggles. Her teeth began to chatter.

Oh, Laura.

They needed to call 911, but as far as she could tell, the man in the kilt had no pockets, just a leather pouch at his waist too small for a cell phone. That left the giantess.

Robbi held up her dripping phone and raised her eyebrows. The giantess—what had the man called her? Joanne?—turned her palms upward and said, "Sorry."

Normally, Robbi would have considered freedom from cell phones a perk of living in a cottage in the woods and wearing costumes with no pockets, but now it just seemed foolish. How would you call for an ambulance if you got bitten by a copperhead?

The man in the kilt said to Joanne, with a hint of a Scottish brogue, "One of us will have to go back up and call the sheriff. Might as well let Guy know, while you're at it."

Guy Cavanaugh, Robbi remembered from Laura's emails, was the owner of the faire. Charming, she'd said. Rakishly handsome. Extremely rich. An incorrigible but lovable cad.

"While I'm at it? Sounds like 'someone's' being drafted."

The tremor in Joanne's voice belied the brashness of her words.

"Well, *she* can't go." He nodded toward Robbi. "She doesn't know where Guy lives. And I'm not leaving you alone with her. We'd have three bodies to deal with instead of one." His voice broke off as he glanced toward Laura's body, still bobbing gently beneath the bridge. "And you can't stay here by yourself. We need to be able to corroborate that no one's touched her, touched anything."

Robbi looked up from her waterlogged phone. He sounded so calm. Too calm. But there was a shimmer of tears in his eyes.

Joanne said, "I know better than to tamper with anything."

"You know Sheriff Hammond," the Scotsman rumbled. "He's been trying to shut us down for the past six months. If he can find a reason to accuse one of us of anything, he will. And it's not like you and Laura were best friends."

Joanne drew in a startled breath. Then her nostrils flared. "But we were friends. And it's not like she didn't dump you for Dale less than a week ago. If I'm a suspect, so are you."

"Maybe so, but I'll have a witness to ensure I don't muck with anything." He dipped his head toward Robbi.

The giantess heaved a sigh. "You've got an answer for everything, haven't you, Mal?"

Robbi searched her memory for some reference to a man named Mal and came up with an offhand comment about a sheepherder who'd spent much of his youth with a grandmother in Scotland. And at Christmas, Laura had mentioned seeing someone special. But Laura had always been reticent about her love life. She'd always said she was afraid to talk about it because that might break the spell. So Laura's failure to mention a relationship with Mal didn't necessarily mean anything. But the idea that Laura had done the dumping was a big red flag. As far as Robbi knew, Laura had never broken up with anyone before. They had left her, every time.

Maybe the breakup had gone badly, and Mal was the one who'd thrown her in the river.

Robbi shivered. Maybe it was neither he nor the giantess. Maybe it was someone else, or just an awful accident. His surprise at seeing Laura's body had seemed genuine. But the thought of being left alone with either of them felt suddenly unappealing.

I can take care of myself, she thought. But it would be harder now, because she'd shown her hand when she flipped Joanne off the bridge. They'd be prepared, instead of expecting her to be defenseless.

Still dripping, she trudged further up the bank and stood in a patch of sunlight, rubbing her arms for warmth. Mal gave her a speculative look, then scanned the area. His gaze skimmed the kestrel carrier and came to rest on the purse she'd dropped near the bridge.

"No luggage?" he asked.

"My car broke down. I had to walk. I was going to have Laura drive me back for my stuff and call for a tow."

He nodded. "Jo, after you call the sheriff, stop by our place and ask Elinore to send along a blanket or something dry for our new friend to wear."

Joanne picked up the corners of her leather blacksmith's apron and curtsied. "Yes, milord. Should I ask the lady Elinore to send along a flagon of ale to slake your thirst? For surely thou art thirsty after such exertion."

"Funny lady," Mal said, dryly. "A blanket will do."

"I'm all right," Robbi said. "I'm drying out already."

His concern for her assuaged her fears, at least a little. It seemed sincere. Almost sweet. Except that Mal must have been cheating on "the lady Elinore" with Laura, if Joanne's accusation about the breakup was true. Which it probably was, since he hadn't denied it. Her train of thought sent a new wave of guilt through her. What kind of person thought about gossip when her best friend had just died?

The kind of person who didn't want to think about what—or who—was under that bridge.

That thought led her back to Joanne's accusation. Maybe Laura's death was just a tragic accident, but if it wasn't, an illicit affair might be a motive for murder.

Joanne started up the bank, legs pumping in long, ground-covering strides. She paused on the bridge to pick up her axe, and Robbi thought she saw the woman's broad shoulders slump. Then her back straightened and she stomped across the bridge and disappeared into the trees.

A soft, warm presence rubbed against Robbi's legs, and she looked down to see the black cat gazing up at her. To keep herself from bursting into tears, she picked him up and gave his chin a scratch.

"Mal, right?" she asked the man in the kilt. At his nod, she said, "I'm Robbi. Robbi Bryan."

"Of course. Laura's friend. She's been talking about your visit for weeks."

The thought made Robbi's throat tighten, so she forced her focus elsewhere. "Mal, whose cat is this?"

"Some bookseller from Alabama. Laura was cat-sitting for her."

"Tammy," she remembered. Laura had found the bookseller

online while searching for a first edition book on Renaissance costuming. The two had struck up a friendship, two red-haired animal lovers with a love of books and history.

"Right. Tammy. The cat's name is Trouble." He bent to pat the pig, who had followed the cat up the bank. "And this is Tuck."

He had a soothing voice, a rich baritone that made her feel a little less awful.

Trying to lighten the mood, Robbi said, "Methinks Tuck is the troublemaker in this crew."

"An unrepentant stealer of grain. And your bird?"

"Falcor. An unrepentant scourge of grasshoppers and mice."

The border collie nuzzled Mal's hand, and he gently rubbed her ears. "This is Miss Scarlett. Scarlett for short. No vices worth speaking of."

The sun had moved, and a patch of light had shifted closer to the kestrel's carrier. With a final stroke, Robbi set the cat down and moved the hawk box farther into the shade.

She looked back at the bridge. From here, all she could see was a corner of the white gown billowing on the water, but she could still see it in her mind, her friend floating on the water with her hair splayed out around her head like a painting of Ophelia.

The thought sent her mind in a new direction. Could Laura have drowned herself? Over this man? Surely not. If she hadn't killed herself over any of the men who had left her before, then surely she wouldn't do it over a relationship she herself had ended.

She turned back to Mal. "What did Joanne mean, Laura dumped you?"

"Joanne was being dramatic," he said. "It was more of a mutual thing."

"And what about Elinore?"

He looked perplexed. "Not really her concern. I mean, she worries over me, I guess, but all big sisters do."

Sister.

Robbi busied herself with Falcor's carrier, confused by her urge to smile. It wasn't because she was interested. She'd just extricated herself from the worst relationship in the history of the world and had no desire to walk that path again. And even if she had been so inclined, Laura had broken up with him for a reason. Maybe he was emotionally controlling. Or maybe he was a cheat. The cute, charming ones almost always were. And she'd had enough of cute, charming men to last a lifetime.

Still, there was something about him. A softness in his eyes, his obvious affection for his dog and his pig. More kind than charming, really.

"I can't believe she's gone," he said. "She was so excited about you coming to work here. Said you'd been best friends since you were wee ones."

"Since third grade." Robbi had been the new kid, just moved to Watertown after her father got a professorship at a nearby university. She could still remember sitting alone on the playground, watching her classmates play a rowdy game of Red Rover, Red Rover and praying no one would invite her to play.

It wasn't holding the line that worried her. She had a grip like a snapping turtle. But she was small and light, which meant that no matter how fiercely she rushed the line, she would find herself hanging over the other team's linked arms like a sheet folded over a clothesline.

A voice had come from behind her. "I hate that game."

She'd turned to face a slender girl with new-penny hair and the brightest green eyes she'd ever seen. The girl held up her hands for Robbi to inspect. "Aren't these the tiniest wrists in the world? Even the little kids can break right through."

"I hate it too," Robbi said. Her heart pounding, she took a deep breath and revealed her status as a misfit. "I'd rather read."

"Reading's the best." The girl held out a pinkie. "I guess we'd better be friends."

And they had been, not just friends but best friends, that year and every year since. Robbi sank to the ground beside Falcor's cage and crossed her arms on top of her knees. Her eyes burned, and her throat felt swollen, but she managed to keep herself from crying.

Mal sat down beside her, arranging his kilt. She felt the warmth of his thigh beside hers, close but not quite touching, and despite her reservations, she was glad for his presence.

To be alone with her best friend's body, that would simply be too awful.

MAL ABSENTLY STROKED Scarlett's ears as the border collie lay on the grass beside him. Tuck rooted nearby for earthworms or mushrooms, while the cat trotted down the bank and sat beside the bridge pilings, staring at Laura's body.

He wondered what the cat was thinking, if Trouble understood that his caregiver would no longer be around to braise fish for his dinner. Mal suspected he did. Animals were smarter than people gave them credit for, and Trouble was an exceptionally clever animal. The last time Mal had spoken to Laura, she'd said, "It's uncanny how smart he is. I swear, last night he changed the television channel to the BBC."

It seemed impossible that she could be dead, when just last night she'd invited him over to share a bottle of wine and a bananas foster crème brûlée with her and Dale. Truth be told, Mal would have preferred a plain banana pudding, but then, he'd never been known for his sophisticated tastes. His ex-wife used to call him a Philistine, which he guessed he was. Only a Philistine, she said, would have any use for haggis.

The woman beside him drew in a quivering breath. Robbi, short for Robyn. Laura had called her the closest thing to family she had left. What a shock it must have been, thinking you were spending the next six months with a friend and then stumbling over her body instead. He wished he could say something to comfort her, but nothing seemed adequate.

He sat beside her in silence until he heard voices coming from the woods across the bridge, Joanne's urgent, Guy's smooth and sincere. Probably thinking about PR, how to assure the public that whatever had happened to Laura was unrelated to her work with the faire. Guy was good at spinning things.

Mal climbed to his feet, smoothing his kilt, and extended a hand to Robbi. Her hand felt cold, and he realized she was shivering. "You going to be okay?"

"I think so," she said. Her gaze drifted to the bank, where the cat had tipped his head toward the approaching voices. "Like Laura would have said, I guess I'd better be."

GUY AND JOANNE arrive and mill about, Guy looking rather green, until the sheriff and his deputies arrive with the county coroner in tow.

After they remove Laura's body from the river, I trot over to her. She's wearing a white silk gown with a full skirt and a fitted bodice. Both are embroidered with ivory roses, each with a tiny pearl at its heart. She's been working on this dress for the past three nights, sewing on the pearls by hand, then holding it up for me to admire as she completed each new section.

"Trouble," she'd said just the night before, "is this not the most beautiful dress you've ever seen? It's going to be my wedding dress, and then I'm going to put it on the cover of my new online catalog."

Batting at a stray length of embroidery thread, I half-listened as she rambled on about the wedding, then shared her plans to subsidize her seasonal Ren Faire income with a high-end custom costume boutique and gift shop. She'd sell her costumes and recipe books, along with imported delicacies from the British Isles. She was talking to herself more than to me, and so my inattention caused me no guilt.

Now, though, I wish I had listened more closely.

Careful not to disturb the scene, I sniff at her sodden gown. It's ruined, marred with streaks of mud and moss. It smells of river water and the lavender soap she wears...or rather, wore. She baked shortbread early this morning, and I catch a whiff of flour and vanilla, but if her killer's scent was ever on her, it has been washed away.

I move to smell her hair and find a nasty wound.

The coroner, an elderly gentleman wearing plastic gloves, glances up and waves me away. "Shoo! Go on, kitty. Get on out of here."

I move a few feet away, uncertain whether I should be more offended by the shooing or by being called 'kitty.' Both, I decide. I sit and lick a paw before sauntering away so he doesn't think he can order me about.

Some people have no understanding of their station in life. There is a reason humans once revered my kind as gods.

Sheriff Hammond and a petite female deputy lean over the coro-

ner's shoulder. The sheriff rubs his chin. "Sad. Musta tripped on that fancy skirt and hit her head."

The coroner squints through his thick glasses and nods agreeably. "Could be, Ham. Unfortunate accident."

The deputy, whom Hammond just calls Debba, shakes her head. "I don't think so." She points to the wound on Laura's head. "Look at the angle of the wound. And it's not like she'd be hiking on treacherous ground, not in these clothes. This doesn't look like an accident to me."

The coroner shifts his attention to her. "Well, now, Debba, you could be right." He takes off his glasses and wipes them on his shirt, peers closely at the wound, then cranes his neck around toward Hammond. "You got a bright one there, Ham. You sure enough do. I think you're looking at a homicide."

From the crime shows I've watched, I know what he should say is that he can't be sure until after the autopsy. Perhaps that's what he means, but he seems a little too eager to accept whatever narrative is set before him.

While Robbi, Mal, and Guy look on, the sheriff sends Joanne with one of his deputies to round up the rest of the Troupe and bring them to the King's Moot, the common hall where he plans to interrogate them. He calls these little chats interviews, but I know what he really means.

I must find a way to listen to these conversations.

CHAPTER THREE

The deputy, a wiry woman with short-cropped sandy hair and a name tag that said *Debba Holt*, was a few inches taller than Robbi, but still had to break into a half-trot to keep pace with Joanne. As Robbi watched them disappear among the trees, Joanne shortened her stride to match the smaller woman's. It reminded Robbi of another childhood game.

Take two hundred baby steps to the end of this path.

Mother, may I?

Yes, you may.

She put her hand over her mouth to stifle an inappropriate laugh. There was something about death that did that to her. At fourteen, she'd had to bite her cheek throughout her mother's funeral to keep from giggling at the preacher's badly knotted tie. When the soloist had warbled out "Amazing Grace" in a tremulous soprano, Robbi had buried her face in her father's handkerchief, shoulders shaking with silent laughter that the other mourners had, thankfully, interpreted as tears.

"It's whistling past the graveyard," her father had said later, when she'd asked him if her laughter meant she hadn't really loved her mother. "It has nothing to do with how much you loved her. Just like blaming me has nothing to do with how much you love me."

But she didn't want to think about that, because she did blame him, she blamed him for everything, and because—as unfair as it was—she loved, had always loved him best.

It took another twenty minutes for the coroner to finish. Robbi watched his every move, feeling more and more nauseated, until Mal took her by the shoulders and turned her around.

"You don't have to see this," he said. "You think you owe it to her, but I'm pretty sure she wouldn't want you to."

Guy nodded and took up a position on her other side. He was as cute as Laura had said, his hair carefully tousled and his dark eyes glazed with what seemed to be genuine shock and sorrow.

The two men kept her occupied with small talk until Sheriff Hammond said, "Okay, let's go," and Robbi turned in time to see that they had placed Laura's body on a stretcher. The coroner zipped up the body bag, and the deputies wheeled the stretcher onto the path and then onto the bridge.

The sheriff shepherded the rest of them across and into the woods on the other side. They walked in silence, and after several minutes the trail split in two. A wooden sign stood at the fork, with arrows pointing left and right. Those pointing left read in calligraphic letters, *King Richard's Tourney Grounds, Jousting*, *Fairy Grove, Living Chess,* and *Herding & Hawking.* The ones to the right said: *Market Road, The Queen's Feasts, King's Moot, Millhouse*, and *Main Stages*.

The deputies and the coroner turned the stretcher to the left, where on Laura's map, another arrow pointing off the page had read, *Employee Parking*. Robbi watched the stretcher disappear around a curve in the trail. Then the sheriff cleared his throat, reminding her that there were other people waiting.

She hurried to keep up with Mal and Guy, thinking that if the situation weren't so serious it would be amusing. With the kestrel in his carrier and the cat, dog, and pig trotting alongside, they could almost be the Bremen Town musicians. They turned to the right, past a row of empty booths fashioned like medieval village buildings and still boarded up for the off-season. Beyond the booths stood a long wood and stone structure labeled *King's Moot*.

Robbi shifted Falcor's carrier to the other hand. He seemed to like the box just fine—raptors often perched in the same spot for hours in the wild—but she'd be glad to get him settled in the mews where he could relax and stretch his wings. As she followed Mal into the room, she sent the kestrel a mental promise: *Soon*.

Inside, Deputy Debba stood beside a massive stone fireplace, one hand resting on the butt of her gun. The expression on her face was earnestly grim, as if she wanted everyone to know she took her responsibilities Very Seriously. There were five others in the room. Joanne sat at a table by herself, while two women and two men perched at another. Tuck wandered over and flopped down at Joanne's feet.

The sheriff, a thin man whose paunch and spindly legs looked like a tennis ball glued to a pair of chopsticks, sauntered to Deputy Debba's side and hitched up his pants. He took off his glasses, the old-fashioned kind with thick plastic frames, and cleaned them on the tail of his shirt before putting them back on. "All right, everybody. If Deputy Debba has done her job properly, you're probably wondering what's going on here. Well, most of you. My guess is, one of you knows full well what this is about. So here's what's gonna happen."

He glared at the group, his gray eyes magnified behind his lenses. "One at a time, each of you is going to come back to Guy's office and answer some questions. Deputy Debba will stay out here and make sure the rest of you don't compare notes." He pointed to a small, round-shouldered man with a balding pate. "We'll start with you."

The little man gave a nervous yelp and looked around at the others, licking his lips. The sheriff beckoned him with an index finger. He swallowed hard and climbed slowly off the wooden bench, as if he were being led to the guillotine.

Robbi arched an eyebrow, Vulcan style, as the black cat fell into step at the small man's feet.

"That's Miller," Mal whispered. "Afraid of his own shadow."

Maybe, Robbi thought. But perhaps that fear was caused by a guilty conscience.

Guy trailed into the office behind Miller and closed the door. That was definitely not standard, but maybe Guy had already been eliminated as a suspect and was now acting as a consultant. That made sense, in a way. It was his faire.

"Let me introduce you to the others," Mal said. "You already know Joanne."

His hand on the small of her back, he guided her to the rest of the Troupe. Deputy Debba edged closer, presumably to monitor the conversation.

Mal pointed to a thirtyish woman in a gray peasant dress

and a tartan shawl. Her hair was dark and curly, and her tentative smile revealed a familiar-looking dimple. Mal said, "My sister, Elinore." He pointed to the other woman. "And this is Cara. That's Cah-ra with an *ah*, not Care-ra with an *ai*. Don't get it wrong, or she'll let you know about it."

She was a stunning woman, with high cheekbones, a perfectly straight nose, and full red lips in a heart-shaped face. Unlike the rest of the Troupe, she wore modern dress. Tight jeans accentuated her curves, and her thick dark hair cascaded across the shoulders of her red silk blouse.

And, lord, the bangles. Bracelets and rings, dangling earrings and strands of gold necklaces. The kind of bling that might have looked tacky on someone else but instead came across as artistic and Bohemian. She met Robbi's gaze and held it with a confidence that said she'd grown up beautiful, the kind of girl Robbi and Laura would have whispered about behind their hands in high school, two plain girls sitting alone on the bleachers. Part envy and part pre-emptive rejection. Robbi felt ashamed of that now.

Mal's voice brought her back. "And this is Dale." He nodded toward a lanky young man with a boyish face.

"Dale Allen," Cara said, flashing the young man a flirtatious smile. "Musician, composer, creator of handcrafted instruments. So, of course, he performs as Alan a' Dale. Really, Mal, are these what you call introductions?"

At Mal's shrug, Cara laughed. "Mal is a man of few words. But let me guess. You're new here. The first of the Seasonals."

Elinore snorted. "You don't have to be psychic to guess she's new. It's not like there are too many of us to count. And she's Laura's friend—we've been hearing about her for weeks.

What we don't know is why she's dragged Sherwood's finest and his lackey in with her."

"I'm Robbi," Robbi said quickly. "Laura—"

Deputy Debba stepped in. "You can't discuss the case."

"Case?" Dale was halfway to his feet when a sharp look from the deputy dropped him back onto the bench. "What does Laura have to do with any case?"

From the table behind them, Joanne said, "We found her in the river, hung up under the bridge. Dale, I'm sorry. Laura's dead."

Mal laid a hand on Dale's shoulder to keep him from lunging across the table. The group broke into startled chatter, and while Deputy Debba tried to regain control, Joanne lapsed into silence.

The deputy slammed her hand down on the table. "That's enough! Next one of you who says a word will spend the night downtown."

MAL CLENCHED his teeth to keep from laughing at the thought of their tiny village square as "downtown." Sherwood, Tennessee was barely a wide spot on the map. The faire was the town's only claim to fame, and when the season ended, the rest of the town hunkered down to wait for the grand opening the following spring. But during the season, it was a heck of a draw. Mal had to give Guy credit for that. He'd taken a forty-two acre plot of forest and turned it into something the whole town could be proud of.

Miller came out of Guy's office, sweating and pale. He scurried to the water cooler by the window and gulped down a cupful, then sat at the other table, as far from Joanne as he could, blinking like a mole in sunlight. Elinore went next, then Dale, who came out looking red-eyed and ashen. He pointed to Cara.

"Guess I'm up," she said blithely, then turned back toward Robbi. "Remind me to read your cards sometime soon."

Mal glanced over at Robbi, who sat straddling the bench, one hand on Falcor's carrier. She looked a million miles away. And no wonder. Poor kid must be exhausted.

Poor kid, huh? He hadn't been thinking of her as a kid when he stared into those incredible brown eyes.

He looked away and headed over to sit beside his sister, giving Dale a comforting thump on the back as he passed. Robbi Bryan was no kid, and whether she was exhausted was no concern of his.

It was just that Galahad complex Elinore had always teased him about, rearing its ugly head. He'd be damned if he'd let it get him into trouble again.

IT WAS cool in the King's Moot, and Robbi's clothes had dried to a clammy dampness. She wished she hadn't said she didn't need the blanket Mal had offered. It was her stupid pride, not wanting to seem needy. If she caught pneumonia, it would serve her right. She rubbed her arms, then her legs, with her palms. All it did was spread the chill to her hands.

Cara came out of the office, as poised as when she went in. She tapped Joanne's shoulder as if they were playing a macabre game of "Duck, Duck, Goose," and Joanne stumped into Guy's office, looking like she wished she could carry her axe. Then it was Mal's turn. He came out and gestured to Robbi with a look she could only describe as fatherly. He couldn't be much older than she was, in his thirties at most, but there was something of an old soul about him, as if some long-ago hurt had attuned him to the suffering of others. He was rooting for her, she realized. The thought made her a little less anxious.

As she reached for Falcor's carrier, Mal said, "I'll watch him for you."

She nodded and made her way to the office, feeling numb.

Guy's office looked like it had been decorated by a group of sixteen-year-old boys with attention deficit disorder. The desk was cluttered with paperbacks, a dragon-shaped pencil holder, a spinning kinetic sculpture made of paper clips, several magnetic sculptures, and a mermaid-shaped tray filled with office supplies. Vintage circus posters, Ren Faire posters, and a map of Middle Earth covered three walls; the other was crammed with newspaper clippings and photos of Guy in costume, either brandishing a weapon or posing with one or several attractive wenches.

Guy-in-the-flesh leaned against the window, petting Trouble, who had hopped onto the ledge. Guy's eyes brightened when Robbi came in.

The sheriff sat at the desk, an open laptop in front of him. He gestured toward an empty chair across from him, and she slid into it, perching on the edge. Her right leg shook, foot bobbing like the needle of a sewing machine, and she pressed down on her thigh to make it stop. Under the sheriff's chilly gaze, she felt as fidgety as Miller.

"Interesting timing," Sheriff Hammond said mildly. His glasses glinted in the light. "You show up just in time to find your best friend's body."

He made air quotes around "best friend."

"Terrible timing." Robbi held his gaze. "Whatever

happened, if I'd been here earlier, maybe I could have stopped it." If she hadn't had to walk those extra miles, if Old Reliable, had lived up to its name...would that have gotten her here in time?

An image of Ophelia flashed through her mind again. Poor, weak Ophelia, drowning herself over that lout, Hamlet. Laura would never have done that, never. She was spunky and strong.

Guy's chair squeaked as the sheriff leaned back in it. "What makes you say that? What do you think happened?"

"I don't know what happened. But if it was an accident, maybe I could have saved her. And if she did it herself, I could have talked her out of it, and if someone else did it, maybe we —the two of us together—could have fought him off. Or her off. Whoever did it."

It had to be an accident. Or maybe a stranger. One of those guys who moved from town to town, preying on pretty young women with big hearts. No one who knew Laura could possibly want to kill her.

Hammond laced his hands behind his neck, and the overhead light reflecting in his lenses turned the glass to silver. She wished she could see his eyes. He said, "We have only your word your vee-hicle broke down."

"You're welcome to try and start it."

"Oh, no doubt it won't start now. Don't mean you couldn't have sneaked in here and killed her, then drove a few miles down the road and sabotaged your car." He looked down at the laptop in front of him, read off the make and model. "I had a buddy used to have one of those. That's a lot of cargo space for a little gal like you."

Her face burned with indignation. Swallowing a retort about the implausibility of her sabotaging her own car, she focused instead on his assessment of her chosen vehicle. In a brittle voice, she said, "I'm a falconer. The back is split into two spaces, half for the falcon and the other half for storage. Coolers for his food, equipment, archery supplies..."

"You're an archer too, huh? I used to shoot at Scout camp. Takes some strength."

She gave an angry shrug. "It depends on the bow."

"To some extent."

She wasn't going to play this game. "What happened to Laura?"

He leaned forward, edging aside a small pyramid of magnetic balls. "Why don't you tell me?"

"Because I don't know. I just looked up and saw her..." Her voice broke, and she turned her eyes upward, blinking hard. "She was just floating there."

Guy pushed away from the wall. "Come on, Ham. You don't really think she coshed Laura in the head and threw her in the river? I mean, look at her."

Hammond did. "A little on the small side, but she's not exactly a Keebler elf. And you heard how she flipped Joanne right off that bridge. She could've done it."

Guy rubbed the cultivated stubble on his chin, as if thinking it through. "Let's say she did do it. Why stage the bit about the car breaking down? She could have shown up tomorrow or a week from tomorrow, and she wouldn't have even been on your radar."

The sheriff blew out an exasperated breath. "Oh, for Pete's sake, Guy, maybe she's just not that smart. And if you can't shut up and let me run this investigation, you can go out there and wait with the rest of them. Truth is, that's where you oughta be anyway. Who's to say you didn't kill Miss Bainbridge yourself?"

Guy sputtered something incomprehensible and propped himself against the window again. In his chagrin, he seemed to have forgotten Trouble, and after a half-hearted bat at his hand, the cat jumped down and strolled over to Robbi. She picked him up, and he settled onto her lap with a dignified meow. She resisted an urge to snuggle him. It might make her feel better, but she could tell by his stately demeanor that snuggling was a liberty she would have to earn.

She found a spot beneath the chin that made him purr, then looked up at the sheriff. "Someone hit Laura on the head? Was that what killed her?"

Hammond shot Guy a reproachful glare, then seemed to relent and heaved a sigh. "Too soon to say without the coroner's report. But it does look like she was hit on the head—or coshed, as my little helper here would say. Some kind of blunt object. Could be that killed her. Or maybe she drowned. She could have gone in anywhere upstream."

Robbi grasped at the sliver of hope. "Could she have slipped and hit her head? Just...fallen in?"

"Accident? Maybe. Or maybe the two of you had a fight, and you hit her, and she fell in. That how it happened?"

He was just doing his job, Robbi reminded herself. She forced her clenched fists to open and said, "I've known Laura since we were eight, and I can count our arguments on one hand and still have all my fingers left over." Sure, they'd sometimes gone their separate ways, both of them busy with school, guys, stuff. But they'd always drifted back again, as close as ever. "We never fought. Never."

"Sure you didn't. I know how girls are. Got two of my own.

Drama." He rolled his eyes. "Best friends today, mortal enemies tomorrow. Next week, best friends again, and in between a lot of crying. Never fought, my eye."

Robbi's eyes narrowed. "Ask anyone. At school, or in our hometown. Teachers. Other kids. They'll tell you."

He threw up his hands. "That's what you wanta go with, I won't stop you. But don't waste my time. Let's go over what happened. Start when you woke up this morning, and don't leave anything out."

She walked him through it, the final packing, loading Old Reliable, the five-hour drive from school with two stops to refresh and refuel, then the fateful clank and rattle as the car gave up its ghost. She dug out the time-stamped service station receipts as she finished with the events at the bridge, then slid them across the desk.

He spent a long time looking at them. Then he pulled a pen from Guy's dragon pen holder and scrawled something across the bottom of each one. "I'll just hold onto these. Evidence and all."

"I'd like a copy, please." She looked at Guy. "You have a copier, don't you? Or a scanner?"

Hammond frowned but didn't protest as Guy moved a wire tree from atop a small photocopy machine. When the copies had been made, the sheriff handed them to Robbi and said, "I'll talk to you again when we get back the autopsy reports and have an official time of death."

Robbi sucked in an involuntary breath. Of course there'd be an autopsy. The thought seemed to leech all the air out of the room.

"Miss Bryan?" Hammond's voice cut through the fog in her brain. "Are you all right?"

"I'm...I'm fine." She stood, forgetting the cat until it launched itself off her thighs and onto the floor.

I'm sorry, Trouble. But I have to get out of here.

Robyn Bryan, more familiarly known as Robbi, is the last of the group to be questioned. I forgive her for unceremoniously dumping me to the floor, as clearly all this has come as quite a shock. And no harm done. I'm exceptionally agile, even for my kind, and stick a perfect landing on all four paws.

I've also managed to acquire a great deal of valuable information by simply trading on my feline charm. While I'm not naturally inclined to be so demonstrative with strangers, you'd be surprised at how effective a rub and a purr can be at lowering a biped's guard. Really, Homeland Security could learn a lot from us cats.

But as I was saying: valuable information. For example, in addition to a wealth of information from the articles on Guy's walls, I learned more about the breakup Joanne mentioned at the bridge. It seems our Laura recently ended a long-term relationship with Mal McClaren in favor of the minstrel, Dale Allen, and that she and Miller have been at odds over a recipe both claim as an old family dish. Miller is an odd little chap, a timid type few human females would find notable at first glance. His teeth practically chattered as the sheriff questioned him, and at least once I thought he might pass out. Whether this was due to a fragile constitution or a guilty conscience is too soon to say.

But Mal and Miller are far from the only suspects. Joanne is noted for her quick temper, and while I've been here only a few days, I've noticed a chill between Laura and Cara. Not even Dale is beyond suspicion. After all, many a murder has been spurred by a lover's quarrel.

I linger as Robbi exits, pretending to clean my paws, in hopes of gleaning one last bit of information from Sheriff Hammond. The door closes behind her, and the sheriff turns to Guy and says, "Well? What do you think?"

"Hard to say," Guy says. "For such a sweet girl, Laura got a lot of people upset."

"How about you?" Hammond asks. "Were you able to get back those shares?"

Guy flushes and averts his gaze. "Not yet."

"Do you know if she had a will? Because if she didn't..." His voice trails off, as if imagining the possibilities.

I roll onto my side and begin to clean my stomach. This has gotten quite interesting.

Guy says, "I've no idea. She's always said she didn't have family. And how many twenty-six-year-olds do you know who have wills?"

The sheriff bares his teeth in a nasty grin. "Then you better hope she doesn't. Because according to your contract, if she doesn't, those shares revert to you."

Guy's look of surprise comes a bit late, and I know he's already considered this. A motive for murder, perhaps? Or perhaps he only thought of it after the body was found and believes admitting it would be gauche.

MAL LOOKED up as Robbi came out of Guy's office. The conversation, which under Deputy Debba's stern watch was confined to small talk, trickled to a halt.

Mal slipped off the bench and filled a cup from the water cooler. "Here." He handed it to her. "You all right?"

She took the water with a grateful smile. After a few sips, her color began to return. "Thanks."

He wanted to ask how it had gone, but the deputy had kept

an iron grip on the conversation and seemed unlikely to loosen the reins now. Instead, he said, "Barring some dramatic confession, they'll probably let us go soon. Would you like me to help you get your things from your car?"

Her eyes brightened, sending a rush of warmth through him. "Yes, please. But I'd like to get Falcor settled in the mews first, if that's okay."

He felt himself grinning, told himself to knock it off. Whatever he was feeling, it was inappropriate under the circumstances. "When I first got into the herding demonstrations, the guy I got Scarlett from showed me the ropes. First thing he told me was, 'Tend to your animals first.'"

She smiled. "My father used to say that too. He was a Master Falconer. I started helping with his birds when I was seven."

The office door opened, and the sheriff sauntered out with Guy in his wake. Trouble trotted behind, looking pleased with himself.

"All right," Hammond said. "We've got a couple of guys searching Miss Bainbridge's cottage. We'll be searching all y'all's places next. Vehicles too."

"Not without warrants, you won't," Joanne said.

Hammond barked a laugh. "Got something to hide, Miss Little?"

A pink flush crept up Joanne's neck. Mal knew she was sensitive about her name. And who could blame her? If she'd been a smaller woman, it might have been endearing, but Mal could only imagine the teasing the big woman had endured over the years. She jutted her chin and gave the sheriff a defiant stare. "I just don't want your grubby hands pawing through my unmentionables."

"She means her Granny panties," Cara said in a stage whisper, and was rewarded by a spate of nervous laughter from the rest of the Troupe.

Hammond said, "I'd'a thought you'd all be anxious to get this thing solved. After all, one of you is probably a cold-blooded killer."

"You can search my place," Dale said. "I don't care."

It should have proven something, Mal thought, but it didn't, because what better way was there for a killer to throw off suspicion—assuming he'd gotten rid of the evidence?

But the sheriff just beamed at Dale and said, "That's the spirit. That's the kind of cooperation that'll help us put whoever did this behind bars."

Joanne said, "You don't even know for sure yet that someone did it. And why are you searching her place without a warrant? The Supreme Court ruled that—"

The sheriff heaved an annoyed sigh. "Miss Bainbridge is deceased, Miss Little. She has no next-of-kin. And that cottage she lives in is part of the faire, which means Guy Cavanaugh owns it. And, just so you don't keep rambling on like a broken record, I'll go ahead and tell you, Guy has given his consent."

He turned toward the others. "So, how about it? Are y'all really going to make me get warrants for all those cottages? If there is a killer, that just gives 'em a chance to destroy the evidence."

While Dale and Cara signed permissions for the search, Mal reached for the falcon's carrier.

Guy beat him to it, his forehead furrowed with concern, and said to Robbi, "The sheriff hasn't finished with Laura's place yet. Do you need a place to stay?"

Robbi's stricken expression told Mal she hadn't thought beyond getting the falcon into the mews and her car looked at.

He put his arm around her shoulders and said, "We're just on our way to get Falcor settled and then pick up her things. She can stay with Elinore and me for a while."

Guy cocked his head with a knowing grin. "Staking your claim already, Mal?"

Mal felt his face go red. He'd overstepped and come off looking like a possessive ass. But Robbi had been through a lot today. Was it too much to hope she could have some time to process it all before a player like Guy moved in on her?

Mal dropped his arm. "I'm not staking any claims," he said, his voice tight.

"Boys," Robbi said lightly, reaching for the carrier. "Enough. Just point me to the mews."

"No, no." Guy handed her the carrier and raised both hands. "I didn't mean to butt in. You two run along and get acquainted." He shot Robbi a charming smile that made Mal want to kick his teeth in. "We'll have plenty of time to get to know each other later."

CHAPTER FOUR

The mews and attached weathering yard were exactly what Robbi had hoped for. Right behind Laura's cottage for easy access, it had a double entrance with a fridge and some shelves for storage in its small foyer, natural grass flooring, plenty of room for Falcor to stretch his wings, a scale for weighing the kestrel twice a day, and a shallow fountain with a constant supply of fresh, filtered water. A small tree stood in the center of the space, with several perches of various heights and diameters scattered among its branches. The combination of wire walls and slatted and solid wood panels gave her bird several places to retreat, room to fly, and a choice of sunlight or shade.

Falcor would feel safe here.

"It's perfect," she said. "It looks brand new."

She slipped on a leather glove, opened Falcor's carrier, and held out her hand. He stepped onto the glove, and she gently placed him on the nearest perch, where he shook out his feathers and stretched. He swung his gaze toward Trouble and

Tuck, who sat just outside the enclosure. Then, apparently deciding they were neither threats nor small enough to eat, he turned his attention back to Robbi.

Mal stood watching, the inner door at his back. "Laura spent days studying YouTube videos and looking at plans. She wanted it to be perfect for you."

Robbi blinked. Laura was good at handcrafts, but hopeless with a hammer. "She built this?"

He laughed. "No way. She wanted it to stand upright. But she supervised every step of the way."

Slowly Robbi turned around, taking it all in. Everything she'd ever said she wanted in a falcon enclosure, here it was. She swallowed the lump in her throat and said, "She always liked to get the details right."

He nodded. "I can't even count the hours she spent researching period patterns and fabrics for her costumes. Or the exact ingredients for a historically accurate recipe. When she did take liberties, she made sure they were well thought out."

"Conceptually accurate." Robbi smiled at the memory. Laura had been meticulous about documenting which of her pieces were authentic replicas and which were what she termed "conceptually accurate" originals.

Mal's sad smile echoed her own. "She'd be glad to know you like this place."

Peeling off her glove, Robbi stepped away from the perch. "It feels weird to talk about her in the past tense."

"Aye, it does."

Falcor cocked his head, fixing a suspicious eye on Mal. Then he shook out his feathers again and flew to the fountain for a drink.

"He looks comfortable," Robbi said. "I've got a cooler of mice and quail for him in the car."

As if there was nothing unusual about a woman with a cooler full of dead mice, Mal fished his keys out of the small leather bag at his waist and said calmly, "Ready when you are."

THE MAN WASN'T MUCH for small talk, Robbi thought, as they made a detour to Mal's cottage to pick up his phone, but the silence felt comfortable. It gave her time to process what had happened, even as the presence of a near-stranger kept her from breaking down. As they hiked past the tourney grounds and through the Seasonals' campground toward the employee parking lot, she thought again how surreal they must look, a woman in khakis and a man in a kilt, trailed by a cat, a collie, and a potbellied pig.

When they reached the lot, Trouble and Scarlett hopped into the cab of Mal's four-door pickup, while Tuck sat on his haunches and squealed until Mal picked him up and set him in the back seat. The pig stood on his hind legs, front hooves on the back of the seat in front of him and looked at the other two animals with a bewildered expression. Robbi could almost see the question on his face: *Why are they up there and me back here?*

Mal gave Robbi a sheepish grin. "I know. I spoil him. At least it will keep him out of Joanne's barn."

Despite—or maybe because of—his obvious affection for a pig, Mal seemed like a nice guy. His grief for Laura seemed genuine, though less intense and less conflicted than she'd have expected from a recently jilted lover. But the flash of possessiveness he'd shown when Guy picked up the hawk box worried her. She'd just gotten free of Jax Connelli, and the last thing in the world she needed to deal with right now was another man who thought he owned her.

As they chatted on the way to Old Reliable, she looked for warning signs. But there were no more red flags, and by the time he'd pulled up beside the car and popped the hood, she just felt grateful for his help.

While Miss Scarlett watched Mal work his magic, Robbi sat on the grass giving belly rubs to the pig. Trouble, of course, was too refined for such familiarity. Tuck had just plopped himself in her lap with a happy groink when the sheriff pulled up and rolled down his window.

Without preamble, he said to Robbi, "Whatever happened to Miss Bainbridge, it doesn't look like it took place at her cottage. There's no reason you can't stay there—unless you're worried about being there alone."

"I'm not worried," she said, though the thought of staying in the cottage without Laura made her chest ache. She knew from experience that a house was never so empty as when someone you loved was missing from it. "Thank you."

He acknowledged her thanks with a flick of his fingers, then rolled up the window and pulled away.

It took Mal another half-hour to get the engine running. Robbi only half paid attention to his diagnosis; like her father, she was non-conversant in the language of machinery.

"The only thing I need to know is whether it's a lost cause," she said. "Or do you think I can keep her running for a few more years?"

Mal shut the hood and wiped his hands on his shirt. "Sure. If by 'running,' you mean sometimes it will work and sometimes it won't. The bright side is, you won't need a car around here 'til the season ends next fall. You can always catch a ride with one of us if you need to run into town." He fixed her with the clearest blue gaze she'd ever seen. "I mean, if you stay."

"I'm going to stay," she said. "At least for now."

She looked away, hoping he wouldn't see the truth behind her words. That she had nowhere else to go.

CHAPTER FIVE

Mal pulled out a few car lengths behind Robbi's mini-SUV, hoping his repairs would hold until they made it back to the faire. Trouble peered back at him from the rear window. Wondering what the cat was thinking, he glanced over at Tuck. There was nothing enigmatic about the little pig. He wallowed happily in the front seat, taking up more and more of the available space until Scarlett's haunches were on Mal's thigh.

"Sorry, girl," he said, and she turned to give his chin an apologetic lick. "I didn't have the heart to put him in the back again, what with all this empty space."

But the drive was short, and they all arrived in one piece, with Robbi's Old Reliable bucking and wheezing its way into the employee parking lot. They transferred her luggage and equipment into the bed of his truck, and she squeezed in beside Tuck, with Trouble on her lap.

Mal took them down the vendors' road past the tourney field and onto what Guy called Cottage Lane and the rest of them called the Loop. Guy's castle stood at one end, with the seven year-round cottages placed at intervals along it, just far enough apart for privacy. The inside of the Loop and the areas between the cottages were mostly forest, cut through with the occasional convenient deer trail.

He turned right and drove the long way around the Loop, pointing out each cottage as they passed. Cara's, with its herb garden and its frilly purple curtains, then the one he shared with Elinore—with the garden, horse barn, sheep enclosure and shearing shed behind—then Joanne's, with her barn and forge. Her Friesian mare, Freyja, looked up as they passed the pasture, then returned to grazing.

Watching the horse, Robbi felt a pang. She hadn't ridden since her sophomore year in college, when she'd lost her childhood mount, a blue roan Arabian she'd called Atreyu, after one of her favorite characters in *The Neverending Story*.

"Laura's house is next," Mal said. "Then Dale's. And then you're back at the castle at the beginning of the Loop."

"What about Miller?" Robbi asked.

"He has a place beside the mill. The new mill, not the old one. Guy built it when he bought the faire. One-stop shopping. Bakery, mill, and living quarters, all in one place."

"Sounds convenient." She scratched the cat's jaw distractedly. "But isolated. Does it ever make him feel like he's...well... not a part of things?"

He hadn't thought of it that way. Miller had been here when Mal arrived, and nothing could have seemed more natural than placing the little man's living quarters next to his mill. He'd assumed Miller had asked Guy to arrange it that way, but it had never occurred to him to ask.

"It's a working mill," he said. "Why trek across country when you can live right there?"

He rolled to a stop in front of Laura's cottage and cut the engine, then shot out a hand to stop her as she reached for the door handle. "Wait."

Crime scene tape, which the sheriff's department must have used to mark off the area, lay in a pile beside Laura's herb bed. The front door of the cottage stood open.

He made it there before her, barely, Scarlett at his heels, and gestured for Robbi to wait until he'd cleared the house. Of course, she entered right behind him, stopping only when she saw the mess inside. The sofa cushions lay on the floor, slashed open, the feather stuffing drifting across the hardwood. The drawers had been upended, their contents strewn around the room. A quick glance into the other rooms—kitchen, bedroom, workroom, bath—showed equal disarray.

Robbi blinked at the chaos. "Do you think the deputies did this?"

He shook his head. "I can't believe this is standard procedure."

"The sheriff didn't seem that keen on standard procedure. Maybe this is his way of making a point."

"Maybe."

Or maybe it was Laura's killer, if there really was a killer, looking for something. If he hadn't found it, he might be back. Or she. No point in jumping to conclusions.

He pulled out his phone and dialed the sheriff's office. The deputy on duty patched him through to Hammond, who grumpily allowed that his deputies might have been a little over-zealous in their search.

"Over-zealous?" Mal tried without success to keep the anger from his voice. "The place is trashed."

"Look, I'll have a talk with 'em tomorrow," Hammond said, and before Mal could answer, he ended the call.

Mal recapped the conversation for Robbi, then added, "Just because it was the deputies who wrecked the place doesn't mean it's safe here. I wish you'd stay with us tonight."

She gave him a tired smile that made him want to pick her up and tuck her into bed. The impulse made his ears grow warm.

"I really need some time alone with all this," she said. "I appreciate the offer. But I think I can handle myself."

He thought of the ease with which this pretty little woman had put Joanne into the water. "I remember," he said, "but I still don't like the thought of leaving you alone here. At least let me check the rest of the house before I go. And take this." He handed her his cell phone. "I have a pager you can call if you need anything."

"A pager?" He could read it on her face: *Who uses pagers anymore?*

"It's been a while since I used it, but it's easy enough to reactivate."

There he went, Galahad-ing again. Elinore would give him all kinds of grief if she could see him now. And he would deserve it. The problem was, he was no longer certain of his own motivations. It had been a long time since he'd felt this kind of attraction for a woman. And that had not gone well.

Not well at all.

WITH MAL GONE, the shadows seemed deeper, the chill in the

air more biting. It wasn't Mal's absence, *per se*, that made the difference, but rather the loss of human contact. At least, that's what she told herself.

Robbi locked the door and, after a quick change out of her damp clothes into sweats and a long-sleeved T-shirt, looked around for a phone. She had Mal's, but that was for emergencies. Surely, this far out in the boondocks, her friend would have a landline. Instead, she found Laura's cell phone on the kitchen counter. She blinked. Shouldn't the sheriff have taken it as evidence? Maybe they'd already downloaded what they needed.

After a moment's hesitation, Robbi picked it up. It was lying in plain view, so surely the deputies had finished with it. And if they hadn't, the time-date stamp would tell them which calls she had made.

She found a search engine icon and looked up Sheriff Hammond's number. When his voicemail picked up on the third ring, she left a message. "I know Mal told you about the mess. I wanted to send you pictures before I clean it up."

She snapped a string of photos of the ransacked cottage and shot them off to Hammond, then rummaged through the cabinets for a bowl and some rice to dry her own cell phone in. She looked at the clock. Barely five o'clock, and already she was exhausted.

Stress, probably. Nothing drained you like anxiety and grief. But it was too early for bed, and beneath the exhaustion she knew she was too wired to sleep. In a way, she was grateful the cottage had been ransacked. It gave her something to do to keep from thinking about her friend's death.

She cleaned up the worst of the mess in the kitchen, then

went out to the mews and weighed and fed Falcor, put the rest of his meat in the fridge, and looked at Trouble.

"How about some supper before we get started on the rest of this mess?" she asked the black cat. At his enthusiastic purr, she turned to rummage through the pantry. It was a modern kitchen, with plenty of counter space and an island in the middle. Robbi recognized a mixer, a blender, and a food processor that looked like something out of a *Star Trek* episode.

Oddly, there was no cat food anywhere, but in the back of a cabinet she found a few cans of tuna fish. They would do until she could get into town and buy some proper cat food. "Sorry, big guy. You can have this tonight, and then tomorrow I'll get you something better."

With an indignant meow, Trouble pawed at the refrigerator, then looked up at her, a knowing intensity in his green-gold eyes. Weird.

But it might be interesting to see what would happen if she went along.

She opened the refrigerator door, and he reached up high to bat at the meat drawer. Smart little guy. "Is this what you want?"

She opened the drawer, watching with amusement as he tapped a package of trout with a paw. It occurred to her that this might seem a kind of madness, taking culinary instructions from a cat. Was Trouble's behavior like the thousand monkeys tapping out the opuses of William Shakespeare? Or maybe she was just distraught and making things up.

Still, what harm could it do to humor him?

Following the cat's lead, she took out two pieces of fish and the butter, then set a cast-iron pan on the stove. She took two bottles from the spice rack and held them up in front of him. Wiggling the bottles, she said, "Well, big guy, which will it be?"

He batted at the hand holding the basil, which she sprinkled lightly on the fish. "Good choice," she said, and placed the turmeric back on the rack. Using the same process, she added a few more spices. A little rosemary, a little lemon pepper.

She set him on the counter while she cooked. When she'd finished, the trout was nicely browned on the outside and flaky on the inside. She looked at the fish, then back at Trouble's expectant face. "Well, I'll be gobsmacked if you don't know exactly what you're doing. I guess this is your way of saying no to ordinary cat food?"

Another meow. Maybe it was her imagination, but she thought she saw a slight bob of his head.

It seemed surreal, this impossible conversation, but only slightly more unreal than Laura's death. She felt like Alice's White Queen, who believed any number of impossible things before breakfast. But she knew what she'd seen, and as her *sifu* would say, things were what they were. Saying they were something else didn't change anything at all.

She set the piece of trout on Trouble's plate, then ate her own standing in front of the stove. She'd washed the dishes and was putting them away when a loud knock made her jump.

She looked at Trouble. "What was that?"

Another series of knocks, louder than before. Then Joanne's voice came from beyond the front door. "Hey, open up! I come in peace."

Robbi hesitated. The big woman had seemed calm enough since her dunking, but clearly she was volatile. Still, Robbi had handled her easily enough on the bridge. Joanne was strong but slow, a combination that made it easier to use her strength against her.

The voice, sounding slightly slurred, called out again. "Oh, come on. I'm tryin' to apologize."

Robbi dried her hands on her pants and went to open the door. Joanne stood on the stoop, her eyes red-rimmed, a wine bottle under one arm and another in her hand. "It's mead. I make it myself. Thought maybe we could—" She stopped, staring at the disaster in the living room. "What in the name of Sam Hill happened here?"

"An overzealous search by the constabulary," Robbi said. "But come on in."

Joanne tromped in past her and flopped down on the couch, seemingly oblivious to the stuffing poking out of a slit in the cushion. "Smells good in here. What's that? Fish?"

"Trout. Trouble and I cooked dinner."

"You and Trouble, huh? Something funny about that cat." She held up the bottle in her hand. "Got a couple of flagons?"

"I saw some mugs in the cabinet."

"Mugs will do."

"And yes, he's really smart. Like, crazy smart."

Robbi fetched two mugs and settled onto the opposite end of the sofa. Trouble sniffed at Joanne's shoes, then retrieved a catnip mouse from beneath the couch and settled onto the loveseat across from them. He held it between his paws, not playing with it, just seeming to savor the aroma while he listened to the conversation.

Joanne filled her mug to the brim, then passed the bottle to Robbi, who poured half a mug for herself. She took a sip, savoring the sweetness of the fermented honey. And something else too, something citrus, and some kind of spice. So much better than beer.

"This is delicious. I tried making a batch like this once," Robbi said. "It wasn't very good."

Joanne chuckled. "The secret's in the aging. This one's infused with orange and cinnamon, so it ages differently. Then there's the yeast. And the way you vent the gases." She stopped, ducking her head as if to make herself smaller. "Sorry. I'm getting carried away. I'm not very good at social talk."

"Social talk is whatever people talk about," Robbi said. "Mead-making counts."

Joanne shot Robbi a grateful smile. "Laura said you were kind."

"I try to be." Robbi tipped her mug, watching the amber liquid gleam in the light. "But then, she was easy to be kind to. Were you two close?"

Joanne took a long pull from her cup. "Not like you two. I liked her. Mostly. I guess she liked me well enough, too. There were times we got on like gangbusters, sharing confidences and such. But she was...you know...a pretty girl. A girly girl. We didn't have much in common."

She drained the mug and poured again.

Robbi took another sip. Now that she knew about them, she could taste the hints of cinnamon and orange. "You must have shared some interests, just being here. The Ren Faire scene is pretty specialized."

"I guess. You've worked faires before?"

"Summers. Nothing like this."

Joanne made an expansive gesture. "This is something special. Guy's little utopia. A group of us stay year-round, keep the place up during the off-season. Then the Seasonals come in, work April through September." She squinted at Robbi and took another draught. "You're early."

"I lost my father. Broke up with my fiancé. I was kind of a mess. So my advisor arranged for me to take some time off from my dissertation, get my head on straight." It sounded so mundane. Such empty words for the complicated mix of adoration, disappointment, and contempt she'd felt for her father, the guilt and grief she'd felt at his loss, or for the disaster that had been her relationship with Jax.

"I was an attorney," Joanne said. She swirled the mead in her cup and took another gulp. "Great in the library, a complete noodge in the courtroom. I knew the other lawyers thought I was a freak, and I'd go into court and fall apart. One day I just walked out. Loaded up my car and drove away. I didn't even know where I was headed, I just drove. Saw a sign for a Ren Faire and thought I'd check it out, and ended up spending most of the day talking to the blacksmith. And that was it. Hooked. I signed on with him that day and spent the next three years on the circuit making swords and shoeing horses. I make a pretty mean suit of chain mail, too."

Robbi tried to imagine Joanne staring down a jury in a power suit and heels. She couldn't fathom it. Not without a wolf pelt around her shoulders and a battle axe in one hand. "How'd you meet Guy?"

"Heard about this place on the circuit and signed on as a Seasonal. He liked my work and invited me to stay." She held the bottle toward the light, watched the liquid slosh around inside. "Great guy, Guy. Gave us all shares in the place and a cut of the gate. Us Rennies, I mean. Bit of a ladies' man, but it's not like he's leading anybody on. Any woman gets involved with him knows what she's getting into. Either that, or she's not paying attention."

"Guy's not your type?"

"And I'm not his." She poured herself another drink, then held the bottle out to Robbi, who tipped her mug to show it was still a quarter full. "Top you off?"

"I'd better not. So, who *is* your type?"

"Ha." Joanne grinned at Robbi, glassy-eyed. Poured the rest of the mead into her cup. "Wouldn't you like to know?"

"Well, I—"

Joanne drained the last of the mead and opened the second bottle. "Doesn't matter anyway. I'm not his type either. Not anybody's, I guess. Think I haven't heard it all—Anvil Amazon. Iron Amazon. Jolly Green Giantess. Guys like him don't go for girls like me. Guys like him don't know girls like me are girls."

Robbi shifted in her seat and tried to look sympathetic. It wasn't hard. As children, she and Laura had both heard their share of nicknames. Half-pint and Mini-me for Robbi, and for Laura, Carrot Top and Pippi Longstocking.

Good times.

Joanne lifted the bottle. "More?"

Robbi held out her cup, and Joanne filled it with an unsteady hand.

"Damn him anyway," Joanne said, eyes brimming. "Him with his dimples and his blue eyes and his sexy little kilt. Him with his conniving little pig."

"Mal," Robbi breathed. "But he and Laura—"

"That's right, he and Laura." Joanne's mouth twisted with grief. "And don't you know my heart broke a little every day to see them laughing and teasing each other? Him fixing her roof and carrying her things like she was made out of porcelain? And do you think she appreciated it one bit? No, she dumped him for Dale and even reneged on the shares she promised she'd sell Mal."

Taken aback by Joanne's obvious resentment, it took Robbi a moment to register what she'd just said. "Wait, wait. What shares? Shares in the faire?"

Joanne had mentioned shares earlier, but Robbi hadn't thought of it as something Laura would have been a part of. But, of course, why wouldn't it be?

The big woman bobbed her head and took another drink. Tears streamed down her cheeks, but whether they were tears of rage or sorrow, Robbi couldn't tell. "That's right. She bought Miller's shares when his mum was in the nursing home and he needed money for her care, and Cara's when her beau-du-jour ran up her credit cards and lost all her savings in a Ponzi scheme, and Dale's—well, just because she asked for them I guess. The deal was, they could stay as long as the faire existed, but if Guy ever sold it, she'd get their share of the profits."

"I don't understand. If you all owned shares, how could Guy sell it without all of you on board?"

"Terms of the contract." Joanne chugged her drink and poured another. "Whoever has the most shares decides if and when to sell, and you'd better believe Guy made sure he had the most. It's legal. I studied the agreement."

"Did you resent that?"

"Why would I resent it? He bought this place. He built it. He keeps things running and pays for the upkeep and the marketing. Outside of our paychecks, he didn't have to give us anything at all. All I'm saying is, Laura was buying up shares willy nilly, and she promised to sell Mal half of what she had."

Robbi frowned. That didn't sound like Laura. Maybe the breakup had been bitter enough to make her go back on her word, but Mal didn't act like a man who'd just been through a bitter breakup. "I don't understand. Why would she back out?"

Joanne hunched a shoulder. "No idea. Something must've happened. Big fight, maybe. Something. Or she died before she got around to it."

Robbi gave Joanne a sharp look. "You seem to know a lot about Laura's business."

"Like I said, we were friends." Joanne's voice broke. "Not best friends, but still...we talked, we sometimes shared our plans. And in a way I loved her, I did. It was just, it was hard to watch how she took him for granted. She didn't treat him like, you know...like a lover. More like a handyman she thought a lot of."

Robbi stared into her cup. Had she almost finished it already? She wanted to defend her friend, but Joanne's words had the ring of truth. Maybe, though, the taking-for-granted had gone both ways. She looked up at Joanne and said, "Why do you think she wanted those shares?"

Joanne blinked. "I don't know. Insurance, I guess."

Insurance. Robbi rolled the word around in her mind. Insurance against what?

THE BLACKSMITH LEAVES, weaving on her feet, a little after midnight. Robbi yawns and says, "Well, Trouble, let's get this place straightened up."

I like this girl. She cooked our trout to perfection—under my expert tutelage, of course—and was quick to recognize my superior intellect. I know it was an experiment at first, that she simply wanted to see what I would do, but that was remarkably open-minded for a biped. Too many humans would have shooed me away from the fridge and dumped a few spoonfuls of canned tuna on a plate for me. Barbarians.

I've nothing against canned tuna. But given a choice, I do prefer a more sophisticated dish.

Robbi finishes up in the kitchen, pitching shards of broken crockery into the dustbin and tucking utensils and intact dishware into the cabinets and drawers. I help by showing her where things go. She straightens the living room, turning the cushions over so the slashes don't show, then moves to Laura's bedroom.

I stay nearby, sniffing for clues. It's a common misconception that dogs reign supreme in the olfactory arena, but with more than 200 million scent receptors, cats can actually detect and discriminate between a wider variety of aromas. Only the true scent hounds have a more powerful sense of smell, but if you factor in the fact that bloodhounds and their ilk are clumsy, drooling, dunderheads, clearly cats are the true victors.

I smell Sheriff Hammond and several strangers—probably the sheriff's crew; Dale and Mal, both regular visitors; Joanne, also a frequent guest; Cara, whom I'd seen leaving in high dudgeon the night before when I returned from a prowl; and Guy, who as landlord might be expected to pop in on occasion. But there is one scent I can find no explanation for. It's an unhealthy blend of flour, sweat, and fear. Yes, the cottage reeks of Miller. It makes me wonder if the scents of flour and vanilla on Laura's body were from something other than the morning's shortbread.

I'm trying to imagine some valid reason for Miller's presence here when Robbi says, "I've found her recipe notebook, but it looks like some pages have been torn out." She holds it up for me to see, then adds, "Keep your eyes open for Laura's diary. She always kept one, and I can't find it anywhere."

Now that she mentions it, I do recall Laura writing in a journal. It was leather, with a flaming phoenix embossed on the front.

There is no sign of it now, but I have an idea where it might be. A few nights ago, she placed some papers in a secret hiding place. Perhaps she put her journal there while I was out. Again, I feel a pang. I should have been there for her.

Robbi sits on the floor and begins to sort through the scattered papers. I meow for her to follow me into the living room, and when she finally does, I scratch at a corner of the Persian rug until I manage to fold it back to reveal the hardwood underneath. The outline of the hidden compartment is subtle, but I can see its shape in a slight gap between the boards. With extended claws, I try without success to lift it. Drat my lack of opposable thumbs!

"What is it?" Robbi asks. "Trouble, stop!"

Then she sees it, the faint square shape concealed by the wood grain. Kneeling beside me, she presses on one corner. Nothing happens, but I think she has the right idea. When she tries a second corner, the opposite one rises. I flip it open with a paw.

"Oh, you clever boy."

Inside is a compartment, a little deeper than a shoebox and wide enough in both directions to conceal a large three-ring binder or a sheaf of papers. But there is no binder. There is no journal either, but there are two pocket folders, one green, one blue. Robbi pulls them out, green on top, and runs a finger across the label. "Sherwood Renaissance Faire Business," it says.

The blue one has a label too. It says, "Last Will and Testament."

Robbi runs her palm across the blue cover. My typically astute powers of perception must be dulled by the day's excitement, because I can't tell if she's overcome by some poignant memory or if she's wondering, as I am, why a twenty-six-year-old single woman in perfect health had thought to make a will. In my experience, humans will do almost anything to avoid confronting their mortality. It usually takes parenthood or a brush with the Grim Reaper to prompt them to set their affairs in order.

Robbi starts to open the folder, then sets it aside with a little hitching breath and picks up the green one. I nudge my way under her elbow so I can read what it says.

Inside are the contracts for Laura's shares in the Ren Faire and property, along with confirmation of the transfers from Miller, Cara, and Dale. Clearly, however, Joanne is only partially in the know, because there is paperwork for the transfer of two more shares. The original owner is listed as Guy Cavanaugh.

So these are the shares Guy and the sheriff were so concerned about. I wonder if these combined shares are enough to give Laura the controlling stake in the faire's fate. If so, did Guy know she had bought the others? Unlikely. Based on Joanne's description of the contract, he had made certain he had the majority of shares. He would surely not have risked selling any had he known they could tip the balance into someone else's favor.

Robbi studies the papers, a small furrow between her eyebrows. Then she slowly closes the green folder and picks up the blue one.

"It's so weird," she says, echoing my earlier thoughts. "It's never crossed my mind to make a will. I mean, isn't that something you do when you're, like, forty?"

I sit back on my haunches, wondering if this is a clue. If Laura had some inkling that her life might be in danger.

"Besides," Robbi adds, "it's not like either one of us has anyone to leave anything to."

I know then what the will says, even before she opens the blue folder. She reads in silence. Then her eyes go wide and her mouth drops open. The blue folder slides to the floor.

"Oh, Trouble." She scoops me up and squeezes me a bit more tightly than I prefer, but sometimes one must suffer for the greater good. "Trouble, she's left everything to me."

I see the implications dawn on her as she gently sets me down and hurries to check all the doors and windows. I don't know if Laura told anyone about her will, or who, other than Joanne, knew she was buying up shares from the other members of the Troupe. Joanne was quick enough to share that news with Robbi, but I don't know the blacksmith well enough to determine whether that was due to grief and alcohol, or whether she is simply prone to gossip.

In fact, I don't know any of these bipeds well enough, an oversight I shall begin to rectify first thing tomorrow morning. Then it will only be a matter of time before I ferret out the miscreant.

I failed Laura, but I shall not fail Robbi.

CHAPTER SIX

She couldn't bring herself to sleep in Laura's bed. Instead, grief and shock kept her awake until well after midnight. Then she slept fitfully on the cot Laura must have set up for her in the workroom. She woke up early to take Falcor for a short hunt in a nearby meadow, then returned to the cottage with her kestrel on her shoulder, only to find Sheriff Hammond and Deputy Debba on the doorstep.

Hammond eyed the falcon warily and said, "Thought I'd come by, see about that mess you and McClaren called about."

Robbi hurried to unlock the door. "I straightened up, but like I said in my message, I took pictures first. I put things away, but I didn't wash anything. And you can see the slashes in the pillows. I didn't fix them. I just turned them over."

"Photos only show so much." He spread his hands. "Wish you'd left things like they were, but there's not much we can do about it now."

That wasn't fair. If he'd wanted her to leave things as they were, he should have told her so—or asked Mal to tell her. But there was no point in challenging him; he didn't seem the sort to take a challenge lightly.

Besides, maybe he was right. Maybe she should have waited.

"Sorry," she muttered sulkily.

The deputy shot her a sharp look, a warning to watch her tone.

Hammond took a short prowl around the living room and stopped on the rug almost directly above the secret compartment. Robbi's heart pounded in her ears like the one in Poe's "The Tell-Tale Heart." Did he know?

He seemed unaware of what he was standing on, but if his deputies had discovered Laura's secret compartment during their search, he might be playing her. She'd learned from sad experience that her ability to suss out a man's deception was her kryptonite.

"So you straightened up," he said. "At least that gave you a chance to look through Miss Bainbridge's things. Anything missing?"

She tried to keep her expression neutral, even though her cheeks burned at Hammond's snide question. Should she tell him about the journal? Or the hidden documents beneath his feet? Years of social programming told her she should confide in him, but her instincts said she couldn't trust him.

She'd just opened her mouth to mention the missing journal when Trouble growled. Startled, she looked over at him. His gaze shifted between her face and the sheriff's, and he growled again, as if he knew what she'd been thinking and was warning her against it.

She almost laughed. But was it really so farfetched? If a cat could cook—or at least supervise—why couldn't one be versed in human behavior?

Okay, big guy. My lips are sealed. For now.

"Is anything missing?" Robbi repeated, cutting off the cat's growl. "I didn't know what was here originally, so it's hard to say."

Sticking as closely to the truth as possible, she added, "We roomed together before grad school, but I have no idea what she might have bought or gotten rid of since then."

He grunted. "Well, keep an eye out, and call if you notice anything suspicious."

She watched them leave, the deputy half skipping to keep up with Hammond's long strides. Deputy Debba hadn't said much, but she didn't seem to miss much either. Robbi hoped the sharp-eyed little woman hadn't noticed she was hiding something.

Her pulse quickened as Hammond turned and walked back up the path. "You should know, our coroner finished his examination this morning."

"Oh?" It was all she could find breath to say.

"Miss Bainbridge died from a blow to the head from a blunt instrument. There was no water in her lungs, so she was dead before she ended up in the river." He glanced at the deputy, his expression grim. "His ruling was homicide."

"Was she...? Did it...?" Robbi couldn't seem to form a coherent thought. She drew in a quivering breath and tried again. "Did she suffer?"

For the first time, something that might have been compassion crossed his face. "Your friend was lucky. He said with the kind of wound she had, she would have died almost instantly."

As soon as the sheriff and his deputy are gone, I make sure Robbi is safe and then head out for a spot of detecting. Unfortunately, the pig, Tuck, is rooting for something at the edge of Laura's garden and spots me. He has taken a liking to my company and, in his mangled Scottish accent, insists on tagging along. He's not a bad little chap, but like most of his species, he's a bit of a plodder. Before I leave, I introduce myself to Robbi's kestrel. He's full of mice and grasshoppers, but while he scans the world outside the mews for prey or danger, I see him take my measure from the corner of his eye. He dismisses me as prey, but unlike Tuck, has no desire for friendship. Nor do I, but he has skills that may yet come in handy. Best make the overture in case they're needed.

My to-do list contains a daunting number of tasks.

1) Find out why Miller was in Laura's house yesterday;

2) Discover why Cara left in a snit the last time she visited;

3) Learn what Guy and Sheriff Hammond know about Laura's acquired shares;

4) Discern more about Joanne's conflicted relationship with Laura, as the blacksmith is tall and strong and could easily have injured Laura in a fit of pique.

I must also investigate Dale, Mal, and Elinore. Mal because of his breakup with Laura and—if Joanne's intelligence is correct—because of Laura's failure to hand over the agreed-upon shares, Dale because the lover is always a suspect, and Elinore because...well, she has as much interest in those shares as Mal does.

I share my plans with Tuck. He suggests we start with Joanne, but the glint in his eyes tells me it isn't clues he's interested in. It's her corn crib. I overrule him, and after a brief pout, he seems to forget his disappointment, trotting along beside me with his usual jovial demeanor.

Although I think Miller a more likely suspect, Cara's cottage is closer, on the far side of the Loop, between Guy's castle and the McClarens' farm. Like the others, it's wood and stone, with shuttered windows and a modern roof made to look like thatch. Tuck and I are aided in my mission because her shutters are open, showing purple silk curtains and cut crystal orbs in various sizes hanging on strings. They sway in the breeze, catching the light. Living inside must be like living in a rainbow.

Beneath the front window is a narrow herb garden, the first shoots beginning to emerge. Already, I can smell the faintest hint of mint. Not for the first time, I revel in the ambience of this place. If not for the recent tragedy, this would be the perfect setting for an Anglophile like myself.

I tell Tuck to stay out of sight. Then I creep to what I surmise is the living room window. I hear Enya music, no other voices.

In back there is a hemlock, the lowest branch of which affords a look into Cara's rear window. From there, I can see past the kitchen and all the way through to the front door, a design that Alabamians call a shotgun house, but which originated in Ireland as a method for outwitting faeries. The reasoning goes that, if the fae enter through one door and can see straight out the other, they'll pass on through without pausing to make mischief. But if both doors don't align, it gives them time to look around—and that gives them ideas. It is never a good idea to give the fae ideas. I have often wondered if they might be part cat.

At any rate, down that long tunnel of cottage, I see the kitchen and living room on the right. To the left is a closed door that, based on the layout of the other cottages, leads to the bathroom and laundry, then an open door to the bedroom. In the living room, a wooden bookshelf filled with New Age titles fills one wall, while the mantel and end tables are covered with crystal balls and a variety of tarot card decks.

Cara is in the living room, dancing, spinning, dark hair flowing around her shoulders, a bangled scarf knotted around her hips. She is a stunning woman, and there is something magical about this wild fusion of Romanian, Middle Eastern, and modern dance. If I were a biped male, I would be utterly enchanted. Fortunately, as a member of a different species, I am able to remain objective.

An elaborate gypsy-style gown in royal purple, with gold trim and a swirling skirt, is draped over one chair. Based on the design and the style of the embroidery, I'm sure it's one of Laura's. Could this be what they argued about?

I am in the midst of devising a fiendishly clever plan for gaining entrance to the cottage when Cara stops dancing and cocks her head as if listening. She turns off the music, and I hear, quite clearly, a grunt from the front of the house.

Did I say grunt? I mean, an oink.

As Cara flings open the front door, I leap from the tree and race for the front of the cottage. Her shriek confirms my fears.

"Tuck! You wicked little marauder! Get out of my rosemary!"

I skid around the corner as Cara runs out, waving her arms and shouting, "Shoo! Shoo!" until Tuck looks up from his rooting with a self-satisfied expression.

For a moment, I think I have a chance to dart inside while Cara is distracted by my hapless partner in crime. Instead, she slams the door behind her and stomps her feet at him until he trundles away.

I crouch beneath the window, muscles bunched, tail lashing, ready to dash inside when she again opens the door. Then she turns and jabs a finger in my direction. "Oh, no you don't. Go on now. Shoo!"

Shoo. As if I were some common pest.

I roll onto my back with a kittenish expression, but she is a canny lass and fails to succumb to my charms.

"I said go!"

With a disdainful look, I stalk away, tail high to hide my injured pride. Briefly, I wish my dad were here. With his Sam Spade persona, he had quite a way with the ladies. Then I realize even the famous

Familiar would be unlikely to thaw this woman. The pig had already poisoned the well.

I find the silly duffer in the woods, still chewing on a sprig of rosemary, with a contented expression that says he's either unaware of or unworried by the fact that he's sent everything pear-shaped. Not only has he let our quarry tumble to our presence, he's alienated her. My whiskers tremble in indignation.

He squints up at me and asks again if we can do our next detecting at Joanne's.

And this gives me an idea. I assure him this is a brilliant plan, and while he gorges on an overturned barrel of corn in Joanne's barn, I slip away to the new mill to do some real investigation.

There are two mills on the property, on separate branches of the river. The path to the Old Mill has a chain across the entrance and a sign that says: Danger! Condemned! Keep Out! A crumbling eyesore from yesteryear, the building is preserved from demolition only by sentiment and a smidgen of historic significance. The river beside it makes it even more unsuitable, as several years ago, a developer artificially diverted part of the waterflow into this branch to create a sluice for kayakers. The whitewater by the mill is treacherous, one of the most challenging in the region, as proclaimed by an article on Guy's office wall. Because almost no one goes there, it's become Guy's favorite spot to practice swordsmanship. He puts in his earbuds and listens to music while going through his maneuvers. I don't know what he listens to, but from his sweeping movements, I suspect it's something epic.

The New Mill, an authentic replica of a gristmill from the Middle Ages, is another matter. With its ever-churning water wheel, it serves as a picturesque backdrop for selfies and wedding photos. Miller's cottage, just a few feet from the mill door, connects to a shop where he creates and sells both sweet and savory pastries and an assortment of other baked goods.

Miller is something of a cipher. I have no idea whether Miller is his given name, a nickname, or a surname, and in the week I've been here, I have never heard him called anything else. His family has been baking for generations, he says. This claim is the root of his feud with Laura.

The day I arrived, she'd shared her third recipe book, Still More Medieval Flavor, *with the Troupe. Miller completely threw a wobbly —or as they say here in the U.S., went ballistic—claiming Laura's recipe for bread-and-butter pudding was his own, a secret passed down through his family since the days of Richard the Lionheart. Of course, Laura insisted that the recipe had passed down through* her *family as well.*

What a foolish, senseless thing it would be if Miller should turn out to be the killer. Of course, murder is always foolish. And this one appears to have been a crime of passion—a quick cosh on the head, most likely in the heat of a disagreement. Which means it could indeed have happened over something as insignificant as a recipe for bread-and-butter pudding.

I can tell right away that Miller is in the shop, because the window is open and a delightful smell is wafting from it. Pastry crust and kidney, if I'm not mistaken, laced with English herbs. I spring onto the window ledge, expecting to see the little baker busy at his stove. Instead, he sits slumped at a long wooden table lined with cooling meat pies. He's staring at a ragged sheet of paper, tears streaming down his face.

Could it be a missing page from Laura's notebook?

I crane my neck to see if I can make out the words, but all I can tell is that there is something handwritten and blurred by tears.

A sharp knock at the door jolts him upright. He shoves the paper into his pocket and wipes his face with his sleeve. As he starts for the door, he sees me in the window and, with a teary laugh, says, "Now, now. That won't do."

He gives me a gentle nudge that forces me to hop out to the ground, then closes the window. The knocking grows more insistent.

Chagrined, I look toward the front door to see who has foiled my attempt to learn the contents of that paper. If this is some trivial matter, the knave shall suffer my wrath.

Naturally, it's Tuck. I'm beginning to see why one might be tempted to go after the wretched creature with an axe.

The door opens, and Tuck looks up at Miller with a goofy pig-grin, one front foot extended in mid-knock. Miller breaks into a grin. "Oh, it's you. You might as well come in." Then, with a wave in my direction, he adds, "And I suppose you might as well come in too."

My whiskers tremble, this time in excitement. Tuck has bumbled our way into the suspect's lair.

MAL KICKED the mud off his boots and shouldered through the screen door on his way to the sink. As he washed the blood from his hands, Elinore looked up from a pot at the stove and said, "Well, doctor, was the operation a success?"

"Mother's grazing, and baby's suckling. No surgery required, just shoved the little one back up and turned her the other way around."

"A happy ending, then."

"Aye, and God knows we could use one." He bent to smell the steam rising from the pot, then pulled back, disappointed.

"Laura, you mean?" She gently stirred the soaking wool with a dye-stained wooden spoon. "I thought you two were on the outs."

He shook the water from his hands and dried them on an embroidered dish towel. "I told you, it wasn't that way. We were friends for two years. You can't be saying I shouldn't miss her?"

"We're all in shock, I think. Of course, you miss her." Elinore rinsed the spoon and tapped it dry on the edge of the sink, then turned the heat down on the burner. "A bit of lunch will do you good. I've still got half of Miller's pie from supper yesterday. We can eat while this simmers."

"Maybe just warm up some frozen fish sticks. I don't feel much like eating anything that came from Miller's kitchen."

Her eyebrows lifted. "You think he did it? Killed Laura?"

"I don't know. There's something off about him. She used to say he stared at her like a croissant someone said he couldn't have."

"He must have had a crush on her, poor thing."

"Poor thing, him or her?"

She shrugged, went to the freezer for the fish. "Both, I suppose. There's nothing pleasant about unrequited love, from either side."

He didn't answer. Both he and his sister knew something about unrequited love. Finally, he said, "You know, I can make my own."

"Don't be silly." She waved him off. "It's no trouble. But speaking of trouble..."

"Laura's cat? I mean, the one she was looking after?"

"No, the other kind." She slid the fish into a pan and turned the oven on. "Salad? Chips?"

"Just fish is fine. What kind of trouble?"

She turned to face him, back against the fridge, her eyes soft with concern. In this light, with her hair to her waist and prematurely threaded with silver, she looked so much like their mother that his breath caught in his throat.

She said, "I saw how you looked at that new girl. Be careful, Mal. Sometimes heartache comes in small packages."

An image of those deep, dark eyes came to him, followed by the memory of how she'd slipped out from beneath his arm. She'd been polite, but that was all. Any spark he'd fancied between them had been nothing more than his imagination.

"You needn't worry on that count," he said, his voice gruffer than he'd intended. "She isn't interested."

"Remind me to be buying you a cup and a cane next time I'm in town." Elinore laid a palm against his cheek. "My poor blind brother."

ALAS, my foray into Miller's shop reveals nothing in the way of evidence. He neither retrieves the paper from his pocket nor confesses his sins over the generous servings of steak and kidney pie he offers us. Naturally, I proceed with caution in case he has laced the pie with poison, but a thorough sniff reveals no untoward ingredients. Since by the time I finish my inspection, Tuck is halfway through his share with no apparent ill effects, I finally partake of the repast. This is why the monarchy employs official tasters.

I must admit, it is delicious. I enjoy a generous serving of the meat and gravy and leave the crust for Tuck. While he inhales my leftovers and a second serving, I take the opportunity to prowl. I find nothing unexpected for a bakery, though there are several areas I'm forced to leave unexplored. The closet doors are closed, and lacking both a human's height and at least one thumb, I'm unable to open them. I manage to nudge open a cabinet door, but before I can properly investigate, Miller pulls me out.

"Time for you lads to go," he says. "I have a lot to do before the Bazaar. I mean, assuming we'll still have one."

Laura told me about this when I first arrived. On the Ren Faire circuit, the Bizarre Bazaar takes place the Monday following an open faire weekend. The vendors trade things like massages, unneeded equipment, services, and whatever else they have to barter. Guy carries the tradition throughout the year: during the off season, the Rennies have one every few weeks. Sometimes it's only Miller selling pies and flour, and the McClarens selling milk and wool. But sometimes everyone brings something. Honey from Dale's beehives; one or two of Elinore's hand-knitted blankets; Cara's candles, skin care creams, and perfumes, all made from essential oils; and occasionally a piece of art or furnishing someone has grown tired of.

Miller shepherds us outside and closes the door behind us. Clearly, there is something in that cabinet he has no wish for me to see. I must find a way to look inside. In the meantime, I shall carry on.

Two tasks down and two to go. I trot toward Guy's little castle while Tuck toddles behind. His feelings are hurt because I left him at Joanne's, but I point out that he was buried to his ears in corn. Was it my fault he was too engrossed in his ill-gotten snack to see me leave?

Tuck is a simple soul, and when I promise not to abandon him again, this mollifies him. By the time we reach the castle, which Guy has dubbed Cavanaugh Castle, or the Laird's Keep, Tuck has forgotten his pique. He rhapsodizes over Miller's pies until, were I less of a gentleman, I would throttle him.

The Laird's Keep is constructed of two circular towers separated by a rectangular living space. My second day here, I slipped inside and found it quite impressive, with a genuine suit of armor, a collection of medieval daggers, and several historic tapestries. The towers were sealed, but an article on the office wall says they are filled with original artwork and collectible replicas from the Middle Ages through the end of the Renaissance. Apparently, young Guy inherited a fortune from his maternal grandmother and used a goodly portion of it to create this little sanctuary.

Tuck and I climb the wide stone stairs and stop before a sturdy wooden door with a lion's head knocker, a handle in place of a doorknob, and a velvet bell pull. One quick leap, and I pull the bell rope, dangling from my claws. A sequence of chimes rings from inside, but no one answers. I drop to the ground and am about to ring the bell again when I hear a faint moan from inside.

Quickly, I confer with my compatriot. Then I climb onto his back and wrap my paws around the handle. My fourteen pounds is not enough to move the door, but it is enough to turn the handle. Tuck, with his greater weight, shoves the door open.

Guy lies just inside the door, an empty glass in his open palm, a sweet-smelling amber pool beneath his hand. Tuck bends his head to lap it up, but I make myself big and drive him away with hisses and fierce yowls. Poor fellow looks terrified, but this is for his own good.

I meow for him to run for help, and he finally toddles down the steps and onto the Loop, his short legs pumping so fast he looks like a wind-up toy. For my part, I fish Guy's phone from his pocket with my dexterous paws. Thank goodness he hasn't password protected it.

There's a red emergency icon in one corner of the screen. I bat at it until a woman's nasal voice says, "What is your emergency?" Then I dash off to Laura's cottage to find Robbi.

There is no time to lose.

ROBBI STOOD BESIDE MAL, watching the paramedics take Guy away on a stretcher, an oxygen mask strapped to his face. Lucky for Guy, he'd managed to dial 911 before losing consciousness, even luckier that Trouble and Tuck had found him and run to fetch help.

The cat's intentions could not have been clearer. He'd yowled at the door until she'd answered it, then tugged at her pants leg and run to the Loop path, where he looked back with an insistent meow that could only mean one thing: *Are you coming?*

She'd seen too much in the past twenty-four hours not to trust his instincts. Resisting the urge to ask if Timmy was stuck in the well, she sprinted after him. Thank goodness she had. By the time she got there, Guy was barely breathing. His skin felt clammy to the touch.

Mal had arrived less than two minutes later, Tuck and Scarlett at his heels. Under Mal's direction, Robbi covered Guy with a blanket and tried to rub the circulation into his cold hands. When his breathing stopped, Mal laced his hands over Guy's chest and pumped while Robbi blew life into Guy's mouth.

It was hard to believe this pale, limp man on the stretcher was the handsome rogue who had flirted with her just the day before.

Robbi rubbed her upper arms as if that might warm the chill in her heart. She looked at Mal. "You seem to know your way around a medical emergency."

"I took a few first aid courses. And I was a vet for a few years, in a previous life."

"You didn't like it?"

"I liked it fine. But I like this too."

She waited for him to explain further. When he didn't, she said, "Is Guy going to be okay?"

"Depends what happened to him."

Robbi rubbed her mouth, then frowned and ran her tongue across her upper lip.

"What's wrong?"

"Something's not right. My whole mouth's tingling." She turned and walked inside, where Trouble straddled Guy's spilled drink, warning Tuck off with a ferocious growl. The pig looked up with a frustrated oink.

Robbi pointed to an amber bottle on the foyer table. "Isn't that a bottle of Joanne's mead?"

With a thoughtful expression, Mal watched the cat guarding the mead. Then he picked up his pig and said over his shoulder, "I think someone had better call the sheriff."

CHAPTER SEVEN

Joanne sat on the jailhouse cot, hands on her knees, head bent. "I swear, I never. Why would I try to kill the guy who gave me a place to live and the best job on the planet?"

Robbi, in a folding chair outside the bars, spread her hands in an "I-don't-know" gesture. "They found hemlock in the bottle, mixed with a strong sedative. Lucky for Guy, the sedative knocked him out before he drank enough to kill him. The bottle was just like the one you brought over the night Laura died."

Joanne moaned. "If I was going to poison someone, I wouldn't use my own mead. I'd put it in one of Miller's pies." Her face brightened. "Hey, if it were me, I'd frame Miller, but if I were Miller, I'd frame me. Maybe that's what happened."

"Maybe." It did seem plausible. There was something ferret-like about Miller. It was easy to suspect him.

"No, look." The big woman stood up, paced her cell. "I kept those bottles in the barn. Anybody could have tampered with one. Or..." Her face paled. "You don't think there could be more?"

"I'm sure they're checking that. You don't have any hemlock stashed in your sock drawer, do you?"

"Poison is a lady's weapon." Joanne did a pirouette, as if to say, *Do I look like a lady to you?*

"Miller's not a lady," Robbi pointed out.

"I know, I know. It was a joke. Mostly. There are plenty of men who poison. But if I were going to kill someone, I wouldn't use poison. I'd bash their head in with an axe."

The image struck Robbi like a boomerang between the eyes. Softly, she said, "That's how Laura died."

Joanne drew in a sharp breath. "Someone hit her with an axe? Please tell me it wasn't my axe."

"She was hit with something," Robbi backtracked. "I don't know if it was an axe."

"Probably not an axe," Joanne said thoughtfully, sinking onto the cot. "Didn't you say the sheriff said it was a blunt instrument? An axe is not blunt."

"Not usually," Robbi conceded. "But point taken. Anyway, I don't think you poisoned Guy, but you've got to give us something we can use to convince the sheriff."

"Us? Who's us?"

"Well...all of us, I guess. Mal, and me, and..." She bit her lip, considering. She hadn't really talked with anyone but Mal.

"Got it, yeah. The bottles in the barn are all I've got. But that's pretty good. It shows accessibility, enough to cast reasonable doubt."

Robbi tried an encouraging smile. "Reasonable doubt is all you need."

"If you get an honest jury, yeah." Joanne sank back against

her pillow. "But they're going to take one look at me and come at me like I'm Frankenstein's monster."

"Come on, Joanne."

"You don't know. You're a little thing. Oh, I know that has its own set of problems. People want to do things for you. They want to treat you like you're helpless. And it drives you crazy."

Robbi didn't answer. She wasn't quite the squirt she'd been as a kid, but Joanne had the gist of it. And it did drive her crazy.

The larger woman went on. "But me, people see me, and they see someone not quite human. Like...a guy threw a cheeseburger at me once. Just rolled down his window and yelled, 'Hey, you stupid cow, say hello to your cousin!' Anybody ever throw a cheeseburger at you?"

Robbi shook her head.

"No, of course not. So when I say I'd never hurt Guy, that's why. He gave me a place where I can be the best damn blacksmith on the circuit and people respect me for it. Where nobody throws cheeseburgers at me."

Robbi nodded, thinking of a quote her father had been fond of: *Be kind, for everyone you meet is fighting a battle you know nothing about.* She wished she'd been better at following that advice.

Joanne sighed. "They can only hold me for seventy-two hours without charging me with something. I hope you can convince the sheriff before then."

"Keep the faith," Robbi said, as Sheriff Hammond poked his head in, rattling the keys.

She was halfway to the door when Joanne called her name. "Robbi? You know the other night? I don't remember everything I said, but...just forget it all, okay? Whatever I said, it was the mead talking."

"No worries." Robbi forced a grin. "To tell you the truth, I don't remember much of it myself."

It was a kind lie, she told herself, as Sheriff Hammond ushered her out and locked the door to the holding area behind her. Even though Joanne's drunken confessions were probably the most honest words she'd heard since she arrived in Sherwood.

THE ATTEMPT on Guy's life changes things. Unlike Laura's murder, which appears to have been a crime of passion, Guy's poisoning was planned. Granted, if Joanne is the culprit, it was a shoddy plan. However, I don't believe that for an instant. Which means it was a crafty plan indeed.

That's not to say she mightn't have killed Laura. It's possible someone else wants Guy dead and is using Laura's murder to cover their tracks. It's also possible that the same person committed both crimes and intends to pin both on our hotheaded young blacksmith. Despite their inauspicious first meeting, Robbi's visit to the jail seems to have convinced her that Joanne is innocent. While I agree, I intend to keep an open mind. In any event, the motive for at least one of these attacks lies with Guy, which means I need to get inside his keep to look for clues.

I shall not invite Tuck. My mission for the evening requires stealth and agility, neither of which are hallmarks of his species. No matter how valiant his heart, poor Tuck shall never climb a tree. I don't even consider approaching Falcor. He could neither carry me onto Guy's parapet nor open the castle door from the inside.

I wait until Robbi is asleep on the workroom cot, then slip out the attic window and climb down Laura's rose arbor to the ground, where I make haste to the castle. I feel confident in my ability to navigate the interior. One of the articles I saw on Guy's wall included a rather detailed floor plan.

The unfortunate thing about weighing a sleek fourteen pounds is the inability to open heavy wooden doors. The good thing about weighing a sleek fourteen pounds is there are few places one cannot find a way into.

In E.A. Poe's masterpiece Murder in the Rue Morgue, *the killer enters the victim's domicile by leaping from the lightning rod onto the ledge of an unlocked window. Guy's castle has a plethora of windows, far too many for even an industrious feline such as myself to test. And, alas, our careless laird has neglected to fit his keep with a lightning rod. There is, however, a convenient sycamore tree from which an athletic young cat might leap onto a parapet. From there, our intrepid hero might climb down one of the great stone chimneys.*

If the chimneys were of brick, I would never attempt it, but Guy's are made of hand-laid stones, which means I have plenty of footholds. Even so, it's treacherous work. The theme from the latest James Bond film plays in my mind as I pick my way downward into the tower on my left, the one referred to in the article as the Great Hall Tower. According to the author, the walls of the hall are lined with period tapestries and iron sconces, while the floors above house one of the country's most extensive collections of medieval and Renaissance art, literature, and artifacts.

I exit the chimney on the upper floor and make my way down the wide stone stairs, my paws still tingling from the strain. It's dark, but the moon shines through the windows, and I have exceptional night vision. What I see are bare floors and walls, the starkness broken by an occasional treasure—a painting by Holbein, an antique spinning wheel, an illuminated copy of a rare Flemish manuscript bound in crimson velvet, each page edged with gold leaf.

Floor after floor, virtually empty, save for what must have been Guy's most valuable treasures.

Tower Two, the Armory Tower, is worse. The only treasures I find there are a dented suit of chain mail and a broadsword proclaimed on the gold plaque beneath to be a Scottish blade from the time of Rob Roy. I can tell by Guy's footprints in the dust beside mine that it has been a long time since anyone else has come here.

Has Guy sold most of his prized collection? If so, I assume it's due to financial difficulties. But why? Bad investments? Mismanagement? Perhaps he's being blackmailed. Or perhaps he's grown tired of the Ren Faire life and is divesting himself of its trappings. I don't believe that for an instant. I've only been here a week, and already it's clear that he loves it too much for that.

I suppose it's possible he's lent his treasures to a museum, but such generosity would likely have been met with more fanfare. By all accounts, Guy is something of a wunderkind when it comes to promoting the faire. It strains credulity that he would pass up such an opportunity for good press.

No, surely whatever has led to these empty galleries has also led to a bottle of mead laced with hemlock.

As I carefully make my way back up the chimney, I feel a swell of accomplishment. Perhaps somewhere on the property, a villain wakes, quivering abed, sensing an impending reckoning.

My father would be proud. I am growing closer.

"FETCH, SCARLETT!" Mal tossed the stick, and the border collie bounded after it with the single-minded focus of her breed. He brushed his hands on his jeans and took in a deep breath. It was a beautiful day, the sunlight slanting golden in the morning mist. The dew soaked his sneakers and cooled his feet; the sun warmed his shoulders through his shirt; and the air smelled of damp moss, hyacinth, and pine. It was almost enough to lighten the pall cast by Laura's death and the attempt on Guy's life.

He followed the Loop past Guy's keep, then strode along the path beside the herding demonstration pens and then the tourney field. Scarlett trotted beside him, occasionally darting away to herd a squirrel or bring him a stick to throw. Occasionally, he'd reach into the pocket of his jeans and slip her a nugget of freeze-dried liver. Just past the tournament field, she stopped short, ears pricked forward.

"What is it, girl?"

He left the path and followed the dog onto a game trail, through a copse of trees, and into an open field. Tuck, lounging in a patch of sunlight, looked up at Mal with a happy snort, while Trouble sat beside the pig, gazing skyward with the intensity of a Jedi master. Robbi stood in the center of the field dressed in jeans and a generously pocketed journalist's vest, swinging what looked like a small leather bat on a string. She moved like the martial artist he knew she was, and for a moment he stood frozen, entranced by her dance with the lure.

She swung it in a figure eight, and a whistling cry turned Mal's gaze upward. The kestrel circled once, then climbed, a small dark silhouette against the blue backdrop of sky. Then, at a short whistle from Robbi, the bird tucked into a dive and plummeted toward the lure. He missed it by a fraction, swooping past her, then tried again for another miss. She whistled again, and on the third pass, he snatched the lure and landed a few feet away, tearing a chunk of raw meat from between the bat's wings.

Robbi walked over and picked him up, the lure line dangling between them as he finished eating from her gloved hand.

Scarlett whined once, and Robbi turned, already beginning to smile. Mal felt a goofy grin spread across his face. He searched his mind for a clever greeting but came up blank.

Beautiful weather? Lame.

Beautiful bird? Made him sound like a suck-up.

How'd you sleep? God no, he'd sound like a lech, thinking about her in bed.

A quote popped into his head, a poem by Yeats he'd learned in Freshman English.

Turning and turning in the widening gyr,

The falcon cannot hear the falconer;

Things fall apart;

The center cannot hold.

Definitely not. Too pretentious. And too much of a downer, in light of recent events.

"Beautiful morning," she said, and he almost laughed at the perfect simplicity of the greeting.

"Aye, it is. Your bird looks good."

Her smile broadened. "We're working on something new. Would you like to see?"

"Of course." Conversation was so much easier when the other person did most of the talking.

She tucked the lure, picked clean of meat, into a pocket of her vest. Then she lifted the kestrel with her gloved left hand, made a circling motion with her right, and launched the bird. The kestrel made a quick, tight circle, then glided back toward

Robbi, eyes fixed on her raised hand. Mal found himself holding his breath.

Robbi turned her palm toward the falcon, and for a moment the bird hovered, his body nearly vertical, wings flapping to hold his position in space. One thousand one, Mal counted. One thousand two. One thousand three. Amazing.

Then Robbi lowered her hand and Falcor fluttered gently to her glove.

"Good boy," Robbi crooned, and gave him another piece of meat from a pocket.

Mal shook his head. "I thought only hummingbirds could hover."

"Kestrels are the only birds of prey that can do it. They're small, but they're full of surprises."

"I can see that." Was she making a comparison to herself? Saying she, like her falcon, was full of surprises? He thought he'd detected a flirtatious note in her voice. Or maybe he was overthinking it. His ex-wife used to say he drove her to distraction with all that thinking.

Robbi gave the bird another treat and said, "I'm glad Tuck's staying out of trouble. Or maybe Trouble's keeping him out of trouble."

"He's definitely a good influence." Mal glanced toward the edge of the meadow, where Scarlett was touching noses with the black cat. "Scarlett will herd Tuck home before long, but he'll slip away when she gets busy watching the sheep."

"Have you tried keeping him penned up?"

Mal laughed. "Can't find a pen that'll hold him. He's a devil with latches and locks. And if you find one he can't open, he'll dig under or break through."

"Free spirit." She gestured for Trouble to follow and started toward the trail. "Were you and Scarlett looking for me? Or did you just stumble across us?"

"Stumbled," he said. "We were out meandering, and she must have heard or scented something."

"Meandering," she said, dreamily. "I love that word. It sounds so...leisurely."

He wondered what she would do if he kissed her. Too soon, he was pretty sure. Not to mention, he'd have to get past Falcor's beak. "Part of our morning routine," he said.

"Speaking of routines. What do you all do with the rest of your day?"

"We all do pretty much our own thing. That's part of the appeal of this place. For me and Scarlett, it starts with a walk. Then breakfast. She and I tend to the flock, then practice herding. Lunch. By then, it's time to find and round up Tuck before he gets himself in too much of a pickle. Sometimes Guy and I practice sword fighting on the tourney field or over by the old mill. This time of year, I help deliver the lambs and kids, shear the sheep, milk the goats, make cheese. Work the horses. Fix whatever needs fixing." He tipped his head toward the falcon. "Don't you need to hood him?"

"Only when it's crowded or noisy. Kestrels aren't as nervous as some of the larger raptors." She gave the bird an affectionate glance. "So...your daily schedule. Does that mean you and Scarlett haven't had breakfast?"

Definitely a flirtatious note.

"Is that an invitation?"

She shook back her hair and gave him an impish grin. "It's an offer to barter. I fix you breakfast, you make sure Old Reliable can get me into town and back."

"Did it give you any trouble when you went to see Joanne?"

"I could hear it thinking about it."

"Would you rather I drove you? Not that I mind fixing Reliable."

"I hate to take you from your lambing. I'm just going to run by the hospital, check on Guy."

Guy. Of course.

There was no malice in her voice, but it felt like a punch in the gut. Not only did she fail to reciprocate Mal's interest, she didn't even seem to know it existed. *She thinks of me as Laura's ex-boyfriend*, he realized. Trying to keep the disappointment from his face, he said brightly, "Biscuits?"

"Sure. I think I saw some jam and honey in here too."

"I'll go get my tools while you fix breakfast." Before she could answer, he turned and strode toward home, kicking himself for his presumption.

So much for a flirtatious tone.

WHEN WE BRITS SAY BISCUITS, we mean cookies, but as it turns out, there were neither. Robbi only knows how to make biscuits from a can, and Laura would never deign to buy canned biscuits. Instead, Robbi makes omelets with mushrooms, peppers, and provolone cheese. She serves them with toast and Laura's homemade peach preserves. For me, she sears a piece of salmon, which I must say tastes delicious.

The tension in the room is thick. The bipeds are clearly attracted to each other—at least, it's obvious to my highly discerning senses—but neither seems willing to admit it. Instead, their fingers brush as they pass bowls and condiments. Despite Mal's palpable disappointment and sense of resignation, to which Robbi seems oblivious, conversation comes easily. They talk about films they loved, like Casablanca *and* Galaxy Quest, *and books, like Stephen Hawking's* A Brief History of Time. *What they don't talk about is their pasts. I catch her stealing glances his way, as if she's trying to figure out what he's thinking.*

Miss Scarlett lies at Mal's feet, her gaze sweeping the room as if, at any moment, she might be called upon to fetch a sheep. She spares a glance of longing at my salmon, then returns to her vigil. I daresay that, with my razor-sharp claws and lightning reflexes, I could successfully defend my treasure, but I'm content not to have to.

For a dog, Miss Scarlett seems a decent sort. Of course, she does smell like a dog. And occasionally, when her instincts as a border collie get the best of her, I must remind her of her place in the hierarchy.

I shall not be herded.

Tuck is outside wallowing in "his" corner of Laura's garden, a patch she planted especially for him. Mal looks out to check on him, then slips Miss Scarlett a bite of egg.

I'm still not thoroughly convinced that Mal is innocent of Laura's murder. His devotion to his animal chums is a point in his favor, but his choice of companions does call his judgment into question. What reasonable person would choose a pig and a dog when he could live with a cat?

Tuck shakes himself off and nibbles at a bit of greenery, then heaves a sigh and lays his head down on his front hooves. Poor fellow. I know he misses Laura. Or perhaps he simply misses the treats she used to make for him. Perhaps, to a pig, it's much the same.

While we eat, I plan my day. I must get inside that cabinet that Miller was so protective of and catch a closer look at the paper he shoved into his pocket. Then I shall investigate the rest of the Troupe.

There is a lot to do!

I'm eager to get at it, yet strangely anxious when, breakfast dishes done and Robbi's car repaired, Mal heads back to his cottage and Robbi drives away. For a moment, I argue with myself. Slip into the car so I can protect her should the killer strike again, or remain behind in hopes of unmasking the foul villain?

I decide on the latter. It will be difficult to follow her into the hospital, and chances are that Guy, if he is Laura's killer, is too weak to do her harm. I know I'm making the right decision. I am a detective, not a bodyguard.

Still, there is a niggle of worry in the back of my mind. I cannot bear to lose another charge.

CHAPTER EIGHT

Sherwood Medical Center was little more than a clinic with a small ER and hospital wing. Robbi found Guy's room easily; there were no wrong turns to take. Guy was propped up in bed, watching a model-thin peroxide-blonde hawking cookware on the shopping channel. It seemed a safe guess that no one had ever thrown a cheeseburger at her. Cara sat in a chair beside Guy's bed, flipping through a New Age magazine and sipping diet soda from a can.

"This is a pleasant surprise," Guy said. He flicked off the TV and pushed himself up further in the bed, his arms trembling with the effort. Cara flipped back her hair and laid a hand on Guy's.

"Be a love," Guy said to her, "and give us a few minutes."

"Of course." Cara's voice was silky-smooth, but she slapped the magazine onto the bedside table as she stalked out.

When she was gone, Robbi said, "I thought I should come and pay my respects."

He gave a weak laugh. "I'm sick, not dead."

"Lucky for you. It's a good thing you managed to dial 911 before you passed out."

"Did I? I don't remember." He leaned back against his pillow, a thin line of sweat forming at his hairline. "I remember dreaming. Something about a cat."

"That was Trouble. He and Tuck found you somehow and ran to Mal and me for help."

A smile played at the corners of his lips. It was a cute smile. "You saved me."

"Well...a little bit, I guess. Mostly, it was Mal. He knew exactly what to do until the paramedics came."

With a wry grin, Guy said, "God bless Mal."

An image of Mal flashed through her mind. Tight jeans. The muscles of his back rippling as he bent beneath the hood of Old Reliable. For a moment she forgot to breathe.

Pushing the vision away, she pulled over a chair and scooted onto it. "Seriously, Guy, what happened? Sheriff Hammond's got Joanne in jail for poisoning you."

"Joanne?" He shook his head. "No, she wouldn't do that."

"Then who?"

"All I know is that my doorbell rang, and when I got there, I found a basket on the stoop. It had the mead bottle in it." He shifted, wincing as the plastic tube tugged at the I.V. needle. "There was no note, so I did assume it was from Joanne. I mean, she makes the stuff."

"Who else would want to kill you?" Robbi asked. "And why? Does it have something to do with Laura's shares?"

His eyes narrowed. "What do you know about those shares?"

"Not much. Just that a lot of people had some. And Laura

had been buying them." She cocked her head. "She bought a few from you, didn't she?"

"I didn't know she was buying them up."

"But she wanted yours, so you had to know it was a possibility. Why take the chance she might end up as the controlling partner?"

He looked away, seeming to study the view of the parking lot through the window. "Laura had a way of knowing a person's weaknesses."

"She was a nice person," Robbi said, an edge to her voice. "It's not—it wasn't—her fault people opened up to her. What I'm wondering is, when you were opening up, what did you let slip?"

He squeezed his eyes shut, then sighed and opened them. "I guess you'll find out soon enough. I can't keep this place afloat much longer."

Robbi bit her lower lip. Laura had said Guy was the richest man she knew. His great-grandfather had made a fortune in the shipping industry, and each subsequent generation had grown their wealth exponentially. The faire had cost a small fortune to build, but Laura had been certain it ran in the black.

"I don't understand. You make a profit every season, don't you?"

He shifted his gaze. Picked at the edge of his blanket. "I've gotten myself into kind of a mess," he said.

When he didn't elaborate, she made a rolling motion with one hand. "What kind of mess?"

"Poker." He couldn't meet her gaze.

She wasn't sure what to say. As awful as Laura's murder had been, it was even more awful to think she might have died over some shares in a worthless enterprise.

"It was innocent at first," he said, as if her silence had given him the strength to go on. "I'd play some local pickup games, and a few times a year, I'd go to Vegas. I'd lose a thousand here, a thousand there. But I was pretty good, so I won more than I lost. Then I got into a high stakes game with some mobbed up guys. I got in deep. Real deep. And I kept thinking, hey, my luck will change. I can still win it back."

"But that didn't happen."

"It didn't happen. And these guys, they don't play around." He finally looked her in the eye. "My granddad used to say credit companies were like loan sharks. They make their profits by making sure you never get out from under. Only difference is, they don't break your knees. Well, these guys do. Or worse. And interest rates? You don't want to know."

"So...you lost all your money gambling, and when it was gone, you sold your shares to Laura."

"Not at first." He lapsed into silence, licked his dry lips.

"Can I get you some water?"

"I'm fine."

"What did you mean, then, not at first?"

"I started selling my collection. Some paintings, some antiques. Good pieces, enough to keep things going for a while. But that's gone too, most of it. Just a few pieces left I can't stand to get rid of." He shook his head and said bitterly. "I pissed it all away."

She gave his hand an awkward pat. He needed comfort, but she needed answers. "You never asked anyone for help? None of the Troupe?"

"What could they do? None of them could come up with that kind of money."

"Joanne said you gave them part of the gate sales. Was that part of the contract with the shares?"

"The shares come into play only if we sell. The split from ticket sales is separate, but it doesn't come to all that much after expenses. Enough to live on, maybe invest or save a little, but trust me, no one is getting rich on it. Even if they were..." He looked away again. "I didn't want them to know I'd let them down."

"If Joanne knew all this, what do you think she'd do?"

He laughed, a quick little laugh that went all the way to his eyes. "Joanne? She'd tie a knot in my tail for sure, maybe even threaten me with that axe. Then she'd give me a thump on the back and buy me a beer. Maybe two. Let's figure it out, she'd say."

Robbi smiled. "She thinks a lot of you too. So for now, let's rule her out."

He made a dismissive gesture, as if he'd already reached that conclusion. "Here's the thing. I got an offer from a developer. A big-time offer, the kind that only comes along when the moon and stars align just right. It's not what I want, and I know it's not what the group wants. It burns our little utopia down to the ground. But it's enough to get me out from under and still leave everyone with a decent stake. If I don't take the offer, we could all end up with nothing."

"Can you sell it without their permission?" Joanne had suggested that he could, but Robbi wanted to hear it from the man who had made the contract.

"The person with the most shares decides. That was always supposed to be me."

"But if Laura was buying shares..."

"Depends on how many she bought."

Robbi looked down at the tiles, that same institutional green she'd seen in her father's hospital room. She shook away the memory and said, "Laura had ten."

He blanched. "Same here."

"And what happens if you die?"

"My shares divide equally among the other share-holders. Mal and Elinore get twice as many, because there are two of them. But..." He broke off. Cleared his throat. "It's more complicated than that."

She touched his wrist. Was she flirting or encouraging? She wasn't sure. She liked him, certainly, despite—or perhaps because of—his flaws. There was something about seeing an attractive man hurting and vulnerable that awakened an impulse she knew better than to give in to. It made her want to fix him.

"You've come this far," she said. "Why not just put it out there? It might help us figure out who tried to kill you. And maybe who killed Laura."

"Hard to believe it's not related," he agreed.

"So..."

He shifted again. Winced again. Gave a small, self-deprecating laugh. "You aren't seeing my best side. I promise, I'm a lot more charming when I haven't just been poisoned."

"Charm is over-rated." She stopped her hand half a second before it reached to smooth her hair, gave herself a stern reminder that just because he was flirting didn't mean she was going to flirt back.

"Is Mal charming?" he asked.

The question caught her by surprise. *Was* Mal charming? She'd thought so at first, but now she wasn't so sure. He was handsome, certainly. The thought of his unruly curls and dimpled smile made her face feel hot. He seemed honest and decent and sometimes adorably awkward. The kind of guy who would fix your car or move your furniture with no strings attached, and the truth was, that very steadfastness terrified her.

She knew what to expect from charming, unreliable men. Her father had been one, and so had her fiancé—though Jax's charm had vanished near the end—and if she gave in to the impulse that attracted her to Guy, she would know exactly what she was getting into. His dark side was right out in plain view.

A guy like Mal, though? Where was his dark side? Her mother's warning rang in her ears: *If a man seems too good to be true…*

He had a quiet energy that made her feel a little too safe and a little too comfortable, but how much of the Mal she'd seen was a mask?

Slowly, she answered, "No. No, Mal's not charming."

Guy smiled as if he'd won a point.

"You said it was complicated," she said, bringing him back to the topic of the shares. "Why is it complicated?"

He took a long breath. He was getting tired; the exhaustion showed on his face.

"Do you need me to leave now, let you rest?" She willed him to say no. A quick shake of his head eased her tension.

"Laura's not the only person I sold shares to. There's someone else, not one of the Troupe. More like a silent partner. And if Laura died without a will, her shares would come to me and he'd get half of those. Yeah, I'd still have more, but he's pushing me to sell, and he can make things very tough if I don't come through for him."

Robbi rolled her lower lip between her teeth. If this silent partner knew that Laura had been buying shares, maybe he'd assumed she didn't have a will. And maybe he'd killed her to put those shares back into play.

Guy's voice broke. "I guess I've made a royal mess of things."

She reached over and patted Guy's hand again. "You have, Guy. I can't lie about that. But it's water under the bridge." An image of Laura's body flashed through her mind, and she wished she'd used a different phrase. Shaking it off, she said, "Right now, we have to find out who tried to kill you and stop them before they finish the job."

CHAPTER NINE

Sheriff Hammond was waiting for her beside Old Reliable. Not just waiting. His furtive expression and the quick bump of his hip against the back door when she said his name told her he'd looked inside.

"Pretty sure I locked that," she said.

"Nah." He leaned against the side of the car. "Door was ajar. I was just making sure everything looked okay. No vandalism or anything. Weird setup for a little gal like you."

"It's for my bird." As she'd explained to him before, she'd used a screen to separate the front seat from the rest of the car, then flattened the back seat and divided the rear two-thirds of the mini-SUV into halves, the driver's side with a perch running end to end for Falcor and the passenger side for storage.

"Right," he said. "Been up to see Guy, have you?"

What did you say to a question that obvious? "For a bit."

"Don't guess you'll be staying, now that your friend's gone."

"Oh, I don't know." Something about his assumption set

her teeth on edge. She liked it here. It made her feel closer to Laura. It got her away from reminders of her life with Jax. And if she were perfectly honest, it didn't hurt that two good-looking men seemed to be vying for her attention. Her self-esteem had taken a beating during the past year and a half, and it was nice to be treated like a bright, attractive woman and not like, as Jax had once called her, "a self-absorbed little witch who cares more for a useless lump of feathers than about being a partner."

The worst part was the fear that it might be true. Sure, she'd helped pay his way through school, and sure, she'd forgiven him twice for sleeping with her so-called "friends," and she couldn't even count the times she'd spent the whole night helping him with an assignment, then dragged into her first class, bleary-eyed, just a few minutes before the undergraduates she was supposed to teach.

But there were also the dinners she'd missed because her kestrel needed to be flown and the Saturday mornings she'd skipped breakfast in bed in favor of archery practice. Did being a partner mean she didn't deserve a life of her own? If it did, then Jax was right. She wasn't cut out for it.

Maybe she really was too much her father's child.

The sheriff was staring at her expectantly. With an apologetic smile, she said, "What makes you think that?"

A muscle in his jaw pulsed. "Seems to me you'd want to high-tail it out of here quick as you can. Not like you've got any ties to this place. Just bad memories, if you were as close to your friend as you say you were."

She clamped her teeth to keep the angry words inside. Finally she gritted, "Sheriff Sensitive."

He shrugged. "They don't pay me to be sensitive. They pay

me to catch criminals. Like maybe a young woman who'd kill her best friend over a few shares in a Renaissance Faire."

Robbi's breath caught. Somehow, he knew about Laura's will. But how? She imagined a deputy finding the hidden compartment, then carefully concealing it again after reading the documents. A trap for her.

He smirked as if reading the question in her eyes. "I talked to Miss Bainbridge's attorney."

"But attorney-client privilege...."

He crossed his arms, still leaning against the driver's side door. "Ends when the client dies. Unless she had an executor or representative lined up who could invoke it for her. Which she didn't."

Robbi didn't answer. She had no idea if this was true, or if, as Laura's beneficiary, she could invoke privilege on her friend's behalf. Joanne might know. Surely, she'd picked that up sometime during law school. But did it matter now? Even if he was lying—or mistaken—she couldn't make him forget what he'd learned.

The sheriff went on. "Something you might want to think about. One person has been killed, another poisoned, possibly if not probably because of those shares. Assuming you're not the killer, the smartest thing you could do would be sell those shares to Guy and go back home."

"Guy can't afford those shares. And even if he could, I wouldn't sell. The Troupe would all lose their homes."

"They're going to lose them anyway. That place is going under. The only question is whether they leave with a sack full of cash or a pocket full of nothing."

She stiffened. "Why do you care so much about these shares anyway?"

"Protect and serve." His nostrils flared. "It says so on my badge. I'd hate to see those folks lose everything."

That was a load of hogwash if she'd ever heard one. Cocking her head, she weighed his words against everything she'd learned. Then she said, "You're Guy's silent partner."

His eyes went cold. "Be careful, little girl," he said.

He was bigger than she was. Much bigger. And he wasn't just a small-town law enforcement officer. In this small town, she knew, he *was* the law. Ignoring the chill shooting down her spine, she stepped into his space, her heart pounding in her ears.

"You're in my way," she said. For a moment, he stared her down. Then, with a chilly smile, he stepped aside. As she climbed behind the wheel, she looked back over her shoulder and added, "And I'm not a little girl."

STILL SEETHING over the sheriff's insinuations, Robbi pulled into the employee parking lot and headed through the Seasonals' campground toward the Loop. Guy's castle looked lonely, even with its ramparts shining in the sun, but she knew that was only her imagination.

As she passed Dale's cottage on the way to Laura's—now her own, she realized with a pang—she found herself turning up the cobbled path to his door. Her pulse quickened. Maybe she was about to meet the man who had stolen Laura's heart. Or maybe she was about to meet the man who had stolen her best friend's life.

He answered on the fourth knock, wearing patched jeans and a stained shirt, a yellow-tinged rag in his hand. He smelled of linseed oil. Probably polishing one of his handcrafted instruments.

He was a medium-sized man with an average build and an open, ordinary face. Medium-brown hair, mud-colored eyes, a shy, sad smile.

"Laura's friend," he said, stepping aside to let her pass. "I'm not dressed for company, but come on in. I'll open a window, get rid of some of this smell."

"I'm used to it," she said. "Sometimes I use linseed oil to finish my arrows."

"Archer. Right." He moved a box of mandolin strings from a chair so she could sit. She perched on the edge, back rigid with tension, trying to look relaxed. "Laura said you were a regular William Tell."

Robbi smiled at the memory, and a little of the tension drained away. "I tried to shoot an apple off her head when we were kids. Hit her square in the middle of the forehead. Thank goodness I used a suction cup and not a real arrowhead."

"She said she had a red circle on her forehead for three days."

She looked around, trying to get a sense of the man. The furniture was functional rather than beautiful, with a large workstation against one wall and a flat-panel TV screen on another. On a table beside the couch, an open bottle of linseed oil stood next to a half-finished hammered dulcimer. It was beautiful, its trapezoidal body sanded smooth, the polished woods gleaming in the light.

"Cherry wood body," he said, following her gaze. "The sounding board is yellow poplar. It can take upwards of a hundred hours to get her oiled. Takes a while to get the wood pores filled."

"Labor of love," she acknowledged.

He twisted the cap back onto the bottle of oil. "Can I get you something? A drink?"

"Whatever you're having."

"Captain Morgan and Coke."

"Sounds fine." While he puttered in the kitchen, she fidgeted in her chair. In light of Guy's poisoning, she wasn't sure it was wise to accept a drink from a stranger. But surely he wouldn't poison her in his own home, when she might have told anyone she was coming here. Still, maybe she should just pretend to sip it.

A row of photos on the mantel caught her eye, and she got up to take a closer look. In one, Dale and a man who could only be his brother flanked an older woman with a brightly-colored scarf wrapped, turban-style, around her head. In the next, the whole Troupe smiled out from a silver frame. Then, Laura and Dale, his arms around her from behind, both laughing. They looked ridiculously happy, his cheek pressed to her flaming curls, the lights of a Christmas tree glowing behind them.

He came out of the kitchen, two glasses in one hand, a liter of Coke in the other, and a bottle of spiced rum tucked under his arm. He fixed the drinks while she watched, then handed Robbi one and nodded toward the Christmas photo. "She looks beautiful, doesn't she?"

"This was taken at Christmas? This past Christmas?"

"The week before. We spent that week in Gatlinburg, then I went on to my brother's and she drove up to spend the holiday with you." His eyes misted. "She didn't mention me?"

"She said she'd been seeing someone. Someone special. But

she didn't want to say too much because she didn't want to jinx it."

And because Robbi had just broken up with Jax. Laura hadn't wanted to flaunt her happiness. This time the stab of guilt made Robbi's eyes burn.

I should have noticed. I should have been a better friend.

"I assumed that was—"

"You assumed it was Mal."

"When did he find out?"

"He knew all along." Dale tilted his hand and watched the liquid swirl in his glass. "I think he knew before we did."

She looked back at the photo, at the joy in her friend's smile, and took a sip of her drink, savoring the sweetness and the spice. "You make it all sound very civilized. But Joanna said—"

"That they broke up a few days ago? I guess that's what most people thought."

"But why? If Mal knew all along, why the charade?"

He downed half his drink and set it on the table, then settled onto the sofa and pulled the dulcimer onto his lap. "Miller creeped her out. Always staring at her like he wanted to chain her up in the basement. Then there was Guy. He's a cool dude and all, but everybody knows what a player he is. He and Cara used to have a thing, and she's still kind of prickly about it. So Laura didn't want to give him any encouragement. She wasn't interested in a fling, and she knew watching him pursue her would just hurt Cara."

That was like Laura, compassionate yet clear-eyed. Robbi took another sip of the spiced cola and felt the warmth spread from her stomach to her head. "But where does Mal come in?"

He opened the bottle and tipped more linseed oil onto the

rag, then stroked a layer of oil across the surface of the instrument. "She and Mal got to be friends. They hung out all the time, talked about everything. And they decided if they acted like they were together, she wouldn't have to worry about other guys. You know." With circular strokes, he began to rub the oil into the wood. "Unwelcome advances. She wasn't looking to hook up with anybody, and he wasn't either. So—"

"Why not?"

"What?"

"Why wasn't he looking to hook up with anybody?"

He gestured with the rag. The spot beneath had taken on a glossy smoothness. "Dude got burned bad. Nightmare marriage, worse divorce. Truth is, though, I still can't believe they didn't go for each other." He looked down at the light reflecting in the burnished wood. "I didn't think I stood a chance."

His voice broke. She wanted to comfort him, but he seemed like a shy guy, and she thought it might embarrass him. "You must have loved her a lot."

"The minute I saw her." His eyes took on a faraway look. "It took longer for her. She's...she was such a bright flame, and I'm just kind of...ordinary. But she heard me sing and play one night, and she seemed to enjoy it. We got to talking about music, and then we started talking about other things. Pretty soon we were getting together almost every day. And then one day she looked at me, and I knew she felt the same way I did. So I asked her about Mal, and that's when she told me about their little ruse." He gave a funny little laugh. "I've never felt so relieved in my life."

He stood up and plucked a CD from a box beside the bookcase. "I wrote a song for her that night. 'Touch of a

Phoenix.' First song on the track. I thought I'd sing it for her at our wedding."

"Wait. Wedding?"

"We hadn't made it official yet. I was supposed to give her the ring after you got here, so we could announce it to everyone at the same time. Now..." He pushed the CD into her hand and sank back onto the couch, rubbing the dulcimer with unnecessary vigor.

"Why didn't you guys come clean once she told you about Mal?" she asked softly. "I mean, with you in the picture, there was no need for the subterfuge."

"We never kept it a secret. But we're both pretty private people, and we didn't make a big deal about it. She kept hanging out with Mal and me, and people just kept thinking they were a couple. I mean, look at him. Who in their right mind would look at the two of us and think a girl like Laura would pick me?"

He didn't say it like it bothered him, more like it was just a fact of life he'd long ago made peace with. Yet, the more they talked, the more Robbi could see what had drawn Laura to him.

He went on. "Eventually, it just started getting silly. A couple of days ago, Joanne said something about the two of them, and Mal said that they weren't together anymore and that she was with me. And there was a little bit of hoopla about that, and then everyone moved on." He swirled his glass and watched the little whirlpool form and fade. "At least, I thought they did."

Robbi leaned forward, cupping her glass with both hands. "What about your shares in the Ren Faire? What made you sell them to her?"

"Sell them?" The surprise on his face seemed genuine. "I gave them to her. And why wouldn't I? Either we'd get married and it wouldn't matter who owned them, or we wouldn't, and I couldn't bear to stay." His gaze drifted toward the Christmas photo with Laura. "I know this is a sappy thing to say, but I don't know how I'm going to live without her."

Robbi nodded, tears springing to her eyes. "Neither do I."

MAL AND LAURA were only friends! Her heart's leap of joy at the thought seemed both premature and inappropriate. She hardly knew the man, and from the sound of things, he had almost as much baggage as she did. Not to mention, she should not be thinking of romance when her best friend had been murdered.

Doofus. She could almost feel Laura's punch on her arm. *Carpe Diem, girlfriend. Carpe every single freaking diem that you're given.*

Of course, Laura would tell her go for it. But the image of her friend drove all thoughts of courtship from Robbi's mind. She'd been so busy absorbing her new reality and wondering who was responsible for Laura's murder and Guy's poisoning that she hadn't even thought of the other implications. Maybe she hadn't wanted to think of them.

Someone had to claim Laura's body. Someone had to make funeral arrangements. Maybe have them play the song Dale had written, have someone read Laura's favorite poem. Someone had to get a copy of the death certificate and notify... who? Laura's bank and creditors, friends from college and the Ren Faire circuit. Those contacts would be in her phone. But who was left to handle those details? No one but Robbi.

But unless Laura had thought to give her that authority, Robbi might not have a legal right to handle any of that. What would happen then?

She'd handled her father's affairs four months ago, after cancer bridged the gulf between them and then ate him alive, but Laura wasn't blood kin. Robbi had no idea where to start.

She pulled up short, halfway between Dale's cottage and her own, clutching the CD he'd given her. Joanne would know. Joanne was an attorney. Maybe she could help with the legalities.

A small voice in Robbi's head said, *What if she's the killer?*

But Robbi didn't believe that. And even if she was wrong, what better way to flush the woman out than to enlist her help? Robbi could continue to investigate her best friend's death, and if she started to get close, the killer, whoever it was, would come after her.

She'd be making herself bait.

She turned the idea over in her mind. It sounded foolish, but what other way was there, really? With Hammond as Guy's most likely silent partner, she couldn't leave it up to the police.

She would try to spring Joanne, and then she'd take whatever steps she needed to claim Laura's body, and then she'd visit the funeral home, and then...

She passed her cottage by. She could look up the local funeral homes on her computer, florists, all of that, but someone local might have better insights into the various options. And Mal had been Laura's closest friend here—at least until recently. He might know others from the Ren Faire circuit she should invite.

Are you sure you don't just want an excuse to talk to Mal? said the little voice in her head. Since it had a point, she didn't deign to answer.

Instead, she quickened her step as she passed Joanne's cottage with its backyard forge now cold, and rounded the curve of the Loop nearest the McClarens' stone cottage. Its shutters were pine green, its door a brilliant red. A thread of smoke rose from the chimney. A Christmas house. The windows were open, white lace curtains rippling in the breeze. Homey.

Twin flower beds flanked the front stoop, and a vegetable garden stretched along one side of the cottage, the first shoots beginning to push through the earth. Beyond the house, a pair of Andalusian horses grazed beside the barn; in a second pasture, lambs and kids gamboled in the grass, returning at intervals to nurse from their mothers. Robbi paused with a silent *squee* to watch the babies frolic for a few moments, then noticed a smaller pen equipped with a child's plastic pool and slide. Its gate hung from a broken hinge. Tuck's enclosure, she surmised. Naturally, he wasn't in it.

On one side of the stoop, someone had stacked a pile of firewood. She stepped past the pile, noting the long-handled modern axe propped against it. Then with a little start, Robbi realized the front door was ajar.

An image of Laura's ransacked cottage flashed through her mind. Then, something worse. What if Mal and Elinore had been inside? Her imagination added two sprawled bodies to the scene.

"Mal?" She hurried to the door and pushed it open wide. Saw a plush gray couch piled high with sweaters and afghans, a matching chair, and a woman in a long brown dress and knitted shawl seated at a spinning wheel in the center of the room.

Elinore looked up, one hand frozen around the fleece she'd grasped from a basket at her feet, the other pinching the length of yarn that ran to the bobbin. Her foot rose from the treadle as recognition seeped into her eyes. "Most of us knock," she said, her slight brogue reminiscent of her brother's.

"Sorry. I just thought—I was afraid..." Robbi waved a hand toward the door behind her. "It was open."

"You thought maybe we'd been murdered in our beds?" Elinore chuckled. The wheel slowed. "Fair enough, but no. Just letting in a little air."

Robbi let out a relieved breath. "It is a gorgeous day out. Is Mal around?"

"Out working with Scarlett. Is there something I can help you with?"

"Maybe." She explained about the funeral, about friends she might notify, about the music and the poetry.

When she'd finished, Elinore stopped the wheel with her fingertips and tied off the loose end of the thread. "Whispering Cedars is the only decent funeral home, and there's a florist on the square called Katye's Petals. I'm afraid I can't help much beyond that. My understanding is that Laura had no family and not a lot of friends."

"I thought she and Joanne were close."

"I suppose. At least, they spent a fair amount of time together before your Laura got her hooks into Mal."

"That's not—" Robbi started.

Elinore waved away her protest. "Not fair. Aye, you're

right. And I know there was no malice in her. I suppose after the debacle with Mal's first wife, I'm a wee bit too protective."

"First wife? How many have there been?"

"Just the one. And what a piece of work she was. Mal and that big heart of his, he let her stomp all over him." Elinore dropped the hank of fleece into the basket at her feet, then stood and wiped her palms on her skirt. Flicked away a stray piece of fluff. "Mal still thinks he's that little geek he was in high school. He never could get used to the idea that he'd grown into a catch. But I'm being a bad hostess. Tea?"

Robbi wasn't sure she wanted tea, but she still had a slight buzz from the Coke and Captain Morgan Dale had given her. If she was going to drive back into town, a little caffeine might not be a bad idea. "Tea would be great, thanks."

While Elinore heated the water, Robbi picked her way around the spinning wheel and the basket of fleece to look at the bookshelf. You could tell a lot about people by the kinds of books they read. Of course, in this case, there were probably two sets of interests at play.

"Cream?" Elinore called from the kitchen. "Of course, cream. And sugar. I'll bring us some shortbread biscuits too."

Cookies, Robbi translated, but whatever you called them, you couldn't go wrong with shortbread.

She ran a finger down the spine of a book on engineering, then another on medieval architecture. On the shelf below sat a row of books on animal behavior and physiology, along with a Chinese puzzle box and a pair of wire kinetic sculptures like the ones she'd seen on Guy's desk. A wooden tray at the end of the shelf held a miniature Rube Goldberg-type contraption, its cogs, ramps, and levers ending with the "capture" of a small ceramic dragon.

"Nosy little thing, aren't you?" Elinore said, making Robbi jump.

Robbi turned to apologize, but found Elinore smiling, holding out a tray filled with shortbread, a tea pot, and the appropriate accoutrements—a pitcher of cream, a jar of honey, two silver spoons, and a pair of sturdy cups.

Robbi pointed to the bookshelf. "Are these Mal's?"

"The animal books are Mal's. The rest are mine."

"These too?" She gestured toward the sculptures. "They look complicated."

"Lots of practice." Elinore shifted the tray into the crook of one arm, moved a basket of yarn from the coffee table to the floor, and slid the tray into the empty spot. "Mal and I have been making traps and puzzles for each other since we were kids."

"Traps?" Robbi looked more closely at the sculptures, then at the wicker puzzle box. She could imagine them as part of a larger Rube Goldberg invention with a human-sized mousetrap at the end.

Elinore pushed aside a stack of folded afghans and slid onto the couch, waving Robbi to the chair across from her. "Once, he pulled up the kitchen tiles," she said. "About a four-foot square. He took it all the way down to the insulation and then tossed a throw rug over the hole. When he called me in, I ran across it and fell all the way through to the apartment below. Scared poor Mrs. Ferguson half to death." She laughed at the memory as she poured the tea, then handed Robbi a cup.

If a man seems too good to be true...So much for Mr. Perfect. "You could have been killed!"

"Aye, but we were quite young. Strong bones, don't you

know?" Elinore stirred a spoonful of honey into her cup, along with enough cream to turn her tea a light tan. "We've always been good at making things."

Robbi patted an afghan draped across the arm of her chair, then made a sweeping gesture toward the blankets and sweaters scattered around the room. So many colors, so many intricate patterns and cables. "You made all these?"

"Design my own patterns too."

Robbi and Laura had tried once to take up knitting. They'd finally managed a few simple squares, which, to make themselves feel better, they'd called potholders.

After a nibble of shortbread, Elinore added, "And I'm working on some larger versions of those sculptures over by the river, big enough for people to climb on. The first one might be ready for the public by the end of the season."

Robbi tried to fathom the scope of such a project. "I can't even imagine.

"Same concept as the smaller puzzles, really." Elinore said. "It's all just math."

Robbi reached for the honey and cream. "I'm hopeless at math."

The back door opened and Mal came in, wearing a blue chambray shirt and a navy blue utility kilt. Nice legs. But damn, he'd looked good in those jeans. He stopped in the doorway, taking in the scene. A half-smile played across his lips, then faded. "How's Old Reliable?"

"Running great!" Robbi said brightly. Too brightly. She ratcheted it down a notch and held up her crossed fingers. "So far, so good."

"Just having a little girl talk, then, are you? I won't keep you from it." He plucked a cookie from the tray and headed toward what was probably his bedroom. It would be a manly room, Robbi thought. Greens and blues, a map of Scotland on the wall, maybe a tartan bedspread smelling of sandalwood. An image of Mal tangled in the sheets made her cheeks warm.

She said, "Your sister has been telling me about the time you almost killed her." At his blank stare, she added, "You know. The hole in the kitchen floor?"

He looked at Elinore, eyebrows raised, a hint of a smile on his lips. "That's not how I remember it. Trust me, she gave as good as she got."

"Actually," Elinore said, "she came to talk to you. She's making arrangements for your friend Laura."

Robbi set her cup down and quickly explained her mission. "I thought you might know some of her Ren Faire friends I should invite...notify, I mean. Some that I don't know. And maybe help me choose some songs and readings."

"You knew her best," he said.

"But you knew a side of her I didn't."

"Dale—"

"I'm going to ask him if he'll play a song he wrote for her." She gave Mal a beseeching look. She simply could not get through this alone. "I know she'd want you to do something too."

He held her gaze a moment longer than he needed to, that clear blue gaze that seemed to bore into her soul. "We'll talk about it. When will the service be?"

"I'll have to ask the sheriff when the...when she'll be released and I can claim her."

Claim her body.

When the body is released.

Why was that so hard to say?

His eyes softened. "Would you like me to go with you?"

She nodded, eyes welling. "Something else too. I want us to get Joanne out of jail."

"We'll take my truck," he said.

Robbi didn't argue. His head would brush the roof of Old Reliable, and his knees would fold up to his chin. Not to mention there'd be no place for Joanne. Or the animals. Somehow she knew they would find a way to be included. "Just let me help your sister clean up here," she said.

Elinore made a shooing motion with her spoon. "You'll do no such thing, girl. Not if you want to get things taken care of before the courthouse closes."

"But—"

"Get along with the two of you. That great giant of a woman's languished long enough."

CHAPTER TEN

It was easier than Mal expected to talk Hammond into releasing Joanne. It was true that there was little evidence against her, but Mal suspected the decision to let her go had more to do with Guy's influence than with Mal's eloquence.

"Thanks, guys," Joanne said. She picked Tuck up and plopped him onto the seat beside her. With a cheerful grunt, he scooted his haunches closer to her thigh and heaved a contented sigh as Mal turned onto the main road and picked up speed. Scarlett, beside the rear passenger-side window, spared a quick glance at the pig, then resumed her vigil, eyes fixed on the landscape flashing past as if keeping a lookout for lost sheep.

Pointedly ignoring her porcine admirer, Joanne finally answered the question Robbi had asked a few moments before. "Three days. That's how long the family has to claim the body before you can step in and make a claim of your own."

"It's already been three days." Robbi gave Trouble's ears an affectionate scratch. "And there's no family. Her parents died when she was a baby."

Mal knew he was imagining it, but he could almost feel her warmth from across the seat. "Raised by her great-aunt, right?"

"Great-Aunt Esther." Robbi looked into the distance with a wistful smile. "She died three years ago. My father used to call her Auntie Mame."

Mal had heard tales of Aunt Esther's adventures. The time she'd taken the girls to India with only a few hundred dollars and a single carry-on each; the time she'd helped them build a go-cart that had won the downhill race at the fair and then crashed into a booth full of plush animals; the time she'd bought a Jeep Wrangler and taken the girls off-roading. That one had ended with the three of them thigh-high in mud, laughing uncontrollably as the abandoned Jeep puttered into a nearby pond. "Auntie Mame?" he said. "More like the Incredible Mr. Toad."

Robbi laughed. She had a nice laugh. Musical and genuine. Then, dreamily, she said, "*The Wind in the Willows*. I love that book. My father used to read it to me."

"Elinore read it to me. Way past our bedtime, under the blanket with a flashlight."

"You two must have been close."

"Peas and carrots," he said. "Mom was sick a lot. El and I took care of each other."

Why had he gone there? It must have been the reference to a childhood favorite. It had lowered his defenses.

"So was my mom. Sick a lot." Robbi looked across the seat at him as if she meant to pursue the subject. Instead, after a searching moment, she looked away and said, "I always thought flashlight reading was the best. You feel like you're getting away with something, but the something is reading, so how bad could it be?" She turned toward Joanne in the back seat. "How about you? Did you have a favorite book when you were a kid?"

Without turning away from the window, Joanne said, "*Johnny Tremaine*."

Mal grinned. "I guess that explains a lot." He'd read that book as a boy, and the memory of the scene where the apprentice silversmith's hand is maimed by molten silver still gave his fingers a phantom ache.

Joanne pushed the pig away again and asked, "Have they finished the autopsy?"

"Sheriff Hammond said the coroner finished his examination," Robbi answered. She repeated what Hammond had told her.

Mal said, "He's probably keeping some things close to the vest. They'll hold something back to help them catch the bad guy."

Robbi picked a piece of invisible lint from Trouble's fur. "Who do you think is the bad guy?"

"Miller," Joanne said at once, just as Mal said, "Deputy Debba."

In the rearview mirror, Mal saw Joanne's eyebrows shoot up. "Deputy Debba? Why?"

"She and Dale dated for a while. Until he lost his head for Laura."

Mal felt Robbi shift her weight on the seat. She said, "He didn't tell me about that. This place is like a reality show."

Mal shrugged. If that meant drama, he guessed she was right. The faire was a retreat, but people brought their baggage with them. Lots of little complications.

Joanne said, "It's a small community. And the faire season is pretty intense. Relationships, drama, it all gets compressed. Shorter and more exaggerated. But I still think Miller is our bad guy. Every time Laura and I were together, we'd catch him staring at her. There's something creepy about him."

"Your turn, Robbi," Mal said. "Who are you thinking?"

From the corner of his eye, he saw Robbi bite her lip. Then she took a deep breath and said, "Sheriff Hammond."

"Hammond?" Joanne leaned forward, resting her forearms on the back of Mal's seat. "Why would he kill Laura?"

"Just a feeling. There's something off about him."

Joanne chuckled. "Won't hold up in court."

Robbi pushed back a stray lock of hair and said, "I think he has an interest in the faire. Guy told me he had a silent partner, someone he'd sold a few shares to. What if it was Hammond?"

Trouble sat up with a stern meow. It sounded like an assertion.

"Back up a minute," Mal said. "Guy said he had a silent partner?"

He supposed it didn't matter. Guy wasn't obligated to inform the Troupe of what he did with his own shares, and he would never sell enough of them to risk losing control over the fate of his little fiefdom. Still, it bothered Mal that Guy had brought someone else in on their deal without consulting the rest of them.

Robbi gave a quick bob of the chin. "He didn't say who, but Hammond seemed awfully interested in those shares."

Joanne sank back with a snort, and Tuck squirmed back onto her lap. "Of course he is. Those shares might be a motive for Laura's murder and the attack on Guy's life."

"All I'm saying is—"

"I'm telling you, it's Miller."

Mal said, "At this point, it could be anyone. If there's a silent partner, it's just as likely Hammond as anybody else."

Robbi shot him a grateful look. Then, blushing, she bent to stroke the cat, a hank of hair the shade of buttered toast falling across her face. There was something about her that made Mal want to slide an arm around her, to protect her from the unknown assailant who might yet prove a danger to them all, or perhaps give her some comfort over the loss of her friend.

Comfort? Really? Is that what you want to give her?

He would have to rein in that impulse. Even if she were interested, even if he could somehow manage to outshine Guy, this was the worst possible time to make a move. You couldn't come on to woman who'd just lost her closest friend. And even if he could, he wasn't sure he wanted to. She drew him to her like a lodestone, and the last time that had happened, he'd wound up with a heart ripped out and scraped empty.

Whatever this was he felt for her, it scared the hell out of him.

THE CAB of Mal's truck has gone silent, except for an occasional grunt from Tuck. Then Mal's cell phone rings, and Robbi plucks it out of his cup holder and hands it to him. It's Guy, ready to check out of the hospital and needing a ride. Where we'll put him, I don't know. Squeezed in between the pig and the dog, perhaps. Miss Scarlett seems devoted to her post, and Tuck seems determined to graft himself onto Joanne.

His devotion to her seems inexplicable, considering she recently threatened him with an axe, but he insists that secretly she loves him. Poor Tuck believes everyone loves him, including the dog, who, in truth, just wants the little blighter to tame his free spirit and stay in his pen where he belongs. That is to say, where his bipeds put him. Miss Scarlett has been thoroughly indoctrinated. But then, such is the nature of dogs.

This is further demonstrated when Guy climbs in and Miss Scarlett scoots over beside Tuck with nothing to show her displeasure but a longing look out the window. Guy asks a bit grumpily if Mal is planning to open a traveling menagerie, but by the time we reach the faire grounds, he seems to have recovered most of his charm. Something is weighing on him, though, perhaps the fact that someone tried to kill him, perhaps the likelihood that "someone" might try again. Or perhaps the future of the faire itself, bound up with the shares he and the sheriff seemed so concerned about.

These things are weighing on me too. I have not yet managed to unmask Laura's killer or whomever poisoned Guy. Yesterday, I slipped inside the bakery and thoroughly explored Miller's mysterious cabinet. Alas, I found nothing but pots, pans, and colanders. Clearly, whatever he was hiding has been moved. He must have realized I was onto him and found another hiding place.

Over the past few days, I have ingratiated myself with him, the result of which has been an utter dearth of information and a generous supply of succulent meats. Perhaps he means to buy my loyalties, or simply to distract me from my task. I shall not falter, though. A world-renowned detective perseveres, even in the face of such sacrifices.

Of course, a world-class detective also never assumes a suspect's guilt. He must look at the case from every angle and consider everyone a suspect until he or she has been exonerated by evidence. To this end, with my faithful Watson in tow (by which I mean my somewhat faithful sidekick, Tuck), I've taken to visiting each cottage daily. You might be surprised at how imprudent humans can become in the presence of animals. They often reveal their deepest confidences in the misguided belief that we cannot understand a word they say.

This insulting delusion of superiority can be exploited by a clever feline. However, thus far, no one has divulged anything more incriminating than the fact that Cara keeps a photograph of Guy in her lingerie drawer, and Dale occasionally wears mismatched socks.

Mal's truck bounces onto the gravel parking lot, and I realize we've arrived back at the faire. Guy climbs out, still looking a bit pale, and asks Mal to gather the Troupe for a meeting in the King's Moot. He has something important to tell them, he says, about the future of the faire.

My ears prick up. Perhaps the killer's reactions to Guy's news, subtle though they may be, will betray the culprit. Fortunately, like most felines, I am exceptionally observant and well-versed in the nuances of human body language. I must remain alert.

ROBBI SLID onto the bench between Joanne and Mal, with a nod toward Elinore on his other side and another to Cara and Dale across the table. She lifted an obligatory hand in greeting to Miller, who was staring in her direction, and he looked away quickly, his ears turning red. Guy stood at the head of the table, smiling like a diplomat who'd just been offered a cockroach at a state function. Or maybe one who'd been caught with his hand in someone else's till.

Guy cleared his throat. "I have something to confess."

He licked his lips, then glanced around the room without meeting anyone's gaze.

"Well?" Joanne said. "Spit it out, man."

Despite a few false starts, it took him less than ten minutes to lay out the situation, from his problem with the mob to the offer from the developers. As he spoke, Robbi watched the faces of the Rennies, their expressions ranging from stunned disbelief to outrage.

"I'm sorry I got in so deep," he finished. "But the fact remains, I have no choice. I have to sell."

"But—" Miller sputtered, his whole head flushing red, "this is our home!"

"I know," Guy said. "Believe me, I do. But it gets worse. I know some of you sold your shares to Laura. Maybe you thought that with her gone, those shares would go back into the pool. That you might still get something out of the sale. They don't."

As Guy's words sank in, the blood leeched from Miller's face, turning him from a beet to a mushroom. "But...but..."

"She left a will," Guy said. "Which means they go to her beneficiary. Robbi, that's you, right? Ten shares."

Robbi's mouth dropped open. How did he know?

An image of the sheriff flashed through her mind, the flint in his eyes as he'd stepped away from her car. *Be careful, little girl.* She couldn't prove Hammond was the one who'd let her secret slip, since there must have been others who knew. Laura's attorney. Maybe Deputy Debba. Maybe even Dale or Joanne. But she'd bet on Hammond. Apparently, confidentiality didn't mean much in Sherwood.

"I'm sorry," Guy repeated. "I really am. The developers want to move on this thing pretty fast, but I promise you, I'll make sure you're all taken care of. I mean, once I get my creditors paid off."

Robbi could almost see him calculating how much he'd have left. How much he could afford to share. What it would be like to go from the kind of wealth that let you acquire a castle full of historical artifacts to the kind where...well, to the kind where you couldn't.

Then a thought occurred to her and she drew in a startled breath. With ten shares, shouldn't she have an equal say in the fate of the faire? Not that she'd made any real decisions yet. Laura's funeral was as far as she'd planned. Sure, it made sense for Guy to assume she'd want to sell, especially if it was true that not selling meant they'd all walk away with nothing, but she would have appreciated some time to think it over. He should have asked her before making his big announcement.

Before she could speak, Mal said, "I have a better idea." His back was rigid, glacier-blue eyes boring into Guy's. "You like to wager. Fine, let's wager."

Guy blinked. "What?"

"A wager. A bet. Your shares against mine. Winner take all."

"Oh, come on." Guy gave a nervous laugh. "What good would that do me?"

"A bigger slice of the pie. Maybe enough to keep a few of those treasures of yours. If you win."

Elinore broke in. "My shares too, Guy. That should sweeten the pot."

A muscle in Mal's jaw twitched, and when he spoke again, his voice came out low and angry. "What's the matter, Guy? Don't think you can win?"

A red wash crept up Guy's neck and seeped toward his hairline. "What sort of wager are we talking about?"

"Three trials. You choose one, I choose one, the group chooses one in case of a tie. I choose equitation."

This time, Guy didn't hesitate. "I choose swordsmanship."

Robbi glanced around the table. The rest of the Troupe looked as off-balance as she felt. Things were moving too fast.

If Guy won, most of the Rennies would lose everything. If Mal won, the faire might recover, but Guy could be killed. Neither option was acceptable. A tap on her knee drew her gaze downward and she found herself looking under the table into Trouble's eyes. He gave her a stern *meow* and another purposeful tap.

She nodded, then surged to her feet. "I want in too."

Mal turned to look at her, ice in his gaze. Then he gritted out, "Of course you do."

The disdain in his voice seemed so unlike him that only the press of the bench against her calf kept her from taking a step backward. It was a tone Jax had used a thousand times, but she'd somehow convinced herself Mal was different.

Stupid. She'd known him less than a week. But the tightness in her throat and the blur in her eyes didn't seem to care about that.

It's okay to feel hurt. Just don't let him see. She lifted her chin and forced steel into her voice. "I want in," she repeated. "And I choose archery."

CHAPTER ELEVEN

It was all Mal could do to stay in his seat until the tie-breaker had been decided. Axe-throwing. Guy had suggested knives, but the group overruled him because it gave him an unfair advantage. Guy was good with blades, but as far as Mal knew, he wasn't known for his prowess with a throwing axe. Neither was Mal, but at least the field would be even.

Unless Robbi was a ringer.

Not that he'd put it past her. He couldn't believe he'd been so stupid, thinking her sweet-girl demeanor was genuine. He should have known. The last time he'd felt this kind of attraction to a woman, he'd married her. Then she'd emptied his bank account and made a false accusation that landed him in jail. She was from a well-to-do and well-connected family, while he was just a small-town veterinarian. *Take a plea*, his lawyer advised. *You'll serve a few years and get on with your life. If you don't....* The slight lift of the lawyer's shoulders told Mal his prospects were dim, but he'd be damned if he'd plead guilty to something he hadn't done.

Three weeks before the trial, she offered to withdraw her allegations in return for their house and almost all the proceeds from the sale of his building and practice. He walked away from their marriage with five thousand dollars, his pickup truck, and the clothes on his back, and he considered himself lucky.

Lucky, too, that Elinore had gotten him on at Guy's faire and invited him to share her cottage.

Just like old times, she'd said. *I mean, the good parts.*

And it had been good. So good that he'd lowered his guard and let himself fall for yet another woman who'd shown herself ready to leave him with nothing.

He could feel her beside him, radiating indignation, as if he were the one who'd shown a monster behind the mask. Avoiding her gaze, he stood up and strode from the room.

No point giving her a chance to twist the knife in his back.

TUCK HEAVES himself to his feet and hurries after Mal and Miss Scarlett. Robbi looks like she's been slapped with a raw fish. I feel indignant on her behalf, but I can't actually blame Mal for being upset. He and Elinore are in danger of losing their home.

As are they all. Glancing around the room, I see shocked faces, angry faces, faces aghast at Guy's revelations. No one looks happy about this.

I'm proud of Robbi for protecting her interests, though now I wonder if I was wrong to encourage her. Her participation in the wager could put her in the killer's crosshairs. Then again, Guy's announcement may have already done that. I suppress an impulse to cuff his ears. What was he thinking, revealing her ownership of Laura's shares?

I suppose it was bound to come out sooner or later, but given a choice, I would have chosen later. For the first time, I wonder if Guy might have poisoned himself. It certainly drew suspicion away from him as a suspect in Laura's murder. Though, if Robbi's suspicions about Sheriff Hammond being Guy's secret partner are true, Guy was never in any danger of being a suspect; the sheriff would have kept him safe.

I must think on this a bit more.

STILL STUNNED by Mal's abrupt departure, Robbi jumped when a hand touched her shoulder.

"Give him time to come around," Cara said. "You have to admit, you threw a bit of a monkey wrench into his plan to save the faire."

Robbi lifted her chin. "Save it? Or take it for himself? Winner take all, he said."

Cara shrugged. "I imagine it's all the same, to his way of thinking. But I owe you a reading."

"I don't really believe—"

"Nonsense." Cara waved away Robbi's objections with one hand and shepherded her out the door with the other. "You can't enter into a competition of this sort without proper guidance from the spirits."

Robbi started to say she didn't believe in spirits, then thought better of it. This might be the perfect opportunity to take the other woman's measure. She might even manage to tease out what had caused the rift between Laura and this sultry enigma.

Robbi glanced behind her. Trouble glided along in their

wake, wearing an expression she could only describe as purposeful. She knew it would sound strange if she said it aloud, but it made her feel safer, knowing he had her back.

"Have you ever had a Tarot reading?" Cara asked.

Robbi shrugged. "A few."

More than a few, truth be told. There was almost always a fortune teller at Ren Faires, and she and Laura had gotten the occasional reading for fun or for clarity. They'd each bought a handcrafted deck one year, and while Robbi had never learned to use hers, it was beautiful, and that was enough.

Cara lifted an eyebrow and waited.

After a moment, Robbi shrugged. "Okay. Let's see what the spirits have to say about all this."

I SLIP IN BEHIND ROBBI, ignoring Cara's disgusted scowl. She closes the door on Tuck, and I catch a glimpse of his face, startled and disappointed, as he skids to a stop not a moment too soon. Inside, in the center of the living room, is a small round table draped with a lace cloth. Rainbows dance across the fabric as a light breeze from the open window weaves among the hanging crystals. Robbi glances around, her face softening with wonder. Then Cara takes a red silk bag from a nearby shelf, gestures toward a straight-backed chair on one side of the table, and slides into the chair on the opposite side.

Robbi takes the seat across from her and watches while Cara opens the bag and slides out a deck of tarot cards. I have no interest in fortune-telling, but even from here, I can see the cards are stunning, lush oil renderings of the iconic symbols. Cara fans them out, and I catch a glimpse of men and women in medieval costume, cups, swords, a tower, a wheel. Then she folds them together, shuffles, and sets the deck in front of Robbi.

"Think of a question or situation you'd like guidance about." Cara says. "Then take a deep breath, focus on your question, and cut the cards."

Robbi picks up the deck and holds it quietly for a moment. Then she sets it on the table and lifts the top two-thirds. She divides the deck one last time, so she has three fairly equal stacks, then puts them back together: middle, left, right. I can't tell what she's thinking.

Cara smiles and shuffles the deck, then peels off ten cards and places them in a pattern I recognize as a Celtic Cross. It's a complex arrangement, though one of the most common. Even I am familiar with it, despite my lack of faith in divination.

Yes, I know. Cats are often associated with the spirit world, and many consider us mystical creatures. This is not entirely untrue. But I am also a rational being, and like the great Sherlock Holmes, a firm believer in the scientific method and forensic science. But I digress.

Cara lays a card on the table in front of Robbi and says, "This covers you."

It's the Five of Cups, whatever that means. Robbi is already nodding, as if it holds some significance for her.

While they talk, I slip into Cara's bedroom and nudge the door shut. Like the living room, it's full of beautiful things. The coverlet is purple velvet, royal purple, complete with a duvet and decorative pillows in scarlet and purple laid over the more ordinary ones. I see more candles, crystals, a brightly-colored scarf artfully displayed on one wall. Against the other is an armoire with scenes from well-known fairytales carved lovingly into the wood.

Beside the armoire is a bookshelf that looks like it's been organized by color rather than by author or subject. I nose open the armoire and find it full of ornate gowns, a variety of modern and period shoes, a modest selection of modern-day clothing, and a collection of scarves. I recognize Laura's trademark embroidery on more than one of the gowns, but I see nothing that raises alarms. The dresses all seem well-made, nothing worth killing for. I rub against some of the softer gowns, then hop out and bump the door closed. I find nothing surprising in her jewelry box or the smaller dresser drawers. A tangle of sparkling jewelry—a less generous soul might have called it gaudy—and a selection of lace and silk unmentionables.

Then I see a small metal lockbox on top of the bookshelf. Bracketed by knickknacks—a Russian nesting doll, a crystal hummingbird—it looks out of place here, like military ordnance in an art museum. It seems to have been closed in haste, a scrap of yellowed paper protruding from one side. If there is anything incriminating here, it must be in that box.

My muscles bunch as I prepare to leap.

"This covers you," Cara said, turning over the card at the center of the cross. "It's your situation right now, in the present. It represents who you are today."

Robbi looked down at the Five of Cups. Three of the five were empty.

Cara tapped the card. "This shows us a scene of emotional disappointment. You've suffered a loss. Well, we know what that means."

Robbi nodded. Laura. But there were two more empty cups. Jax and her father?

"You're probably focusing on the empty cups," Cara said, as if reading Robbi's mind. "But there are still two full ones. That could mean there's still a chance of happiness or fulfillment, or maybe an inheritance, but one that doesn't live up to your expectations."

"The shares, I guess." You couldn't say they hadn't lived up to expectations, since Robbi hadn't been expecting them at all, but if you looked at it a different way, it worked. She'd expected an extended and pleasurable visit with her best friend, and instead she'd ended up with ten shares in a Ren Faire she didn't care about and which could get her killed.

That was how it was with tarot readings. It didn't matter much which cards came up. It was figuring out how to apply the symbols to your life that helped you clarify your thoughts.

She looked up at Cara. "Were you ever sorry you'd sold yours to Laura?"

Cara hesitated, one hand hovering over the second card. Then she turned it over and laid it across and perpendicular to the first. "This crosses you."

"Cara. The shares?"

"I was in a bind. Laura got me out of it." She gave a bitter laugh. "Apparently, I have a habit of choosing the wrong men."

"That's one thing we have in common." A thought occurred to her. "Why didn't you just ask her to lend you the money?"

A muscle twitched in Cara's jaw. "I did. She wanted the shares. She was afraid I'd throw mine in with Guy if he decided to sell."

"Would you have?"

"I don't know. Maybe." She tapped the card and repeated, "This crosses you."

For a moment, Robbi held her gaze. When it was clear that Cara had said everything she planned to say about the shares, Robbi sighed and looked down at the card. The Five of Wands, a group of young men who seemed to be playing a competitive game. It was upside down. Cara blinked at it a moment before speaking. "This is your immediate challenge. Right side up, it means some kind of competition. The tournament, obviously. But since it's reversed, it's also a warning that your adversaries might ambush or attack you. Or cheat, I suppose."

"Do you think Guy or Mal would cheat? Or attack? I mean, Mal was awfully angry, but..."

Cara lifted a shoulder. "People do strange things when they get desperate. But maybe it's not a tournament adversary. Maybe it's the killer. Assuming that's not one of them too. Let's see if we can get some clarification."

She turned over more cards. In the past positions were the Tower, reversed, and the Three of Swords. Avoiding a necessary change and confronting separation and loss.

It was true. Robbi had avoided confrontations with both Jax and her father, and for different reasons, had lost them both. Wrinkling her nose, she said, "This isn't the most fun reading I've ever had."

Cara gave her a stiff smile that was probably meant to be encouraging. "Looks like you've been going through a rough patch. Let's see if things are looking up."

In the future position, she revealed the High Priestess, reversed. Important information, hidden or obscured. Then, the Two of Cups as a possible outcome. A new friendship or romance.

Robbi grimaced. Friendship was fine, if you knew who to trust. But the thought of a new romance, which had seemed exciting just a few hours ago, now left a sour taste in her mouth.

The rest of the reading was no better: obstruction, enemies in the shadows, fear of loss, the unveiling of uncomfortable truths, a need to muster all her courage to overcome the forces amassing against her. It might all be true, but Robbi didn't need the spirits to tell her she was in a dangerous place, surrounded by people with no reason to wish her well.

Cara touched the edge of the last card with her fingertips. "The final outcome," she said. "You ready for this?"

"What's the best card?"

"For you? The Knight of Cups. Your Prince Charming." At Robbi's expression, she laughed. "Or, if you've had your fill of princes, just the understanding of how to manifest your fondest dreams."

"Fondest dreams sound good." Robbi fixed her gaze on the final card as if she could will the Knight of Cups onto its face. She'd felt adrift for so long, it would be nice to find the path to her fondest dream. Or even to clarify what that dream was. "Let's do it."

Cara turned over the last card, and Robbi stared down in dismay at the waving black banner and the helmed skull grinning up at her.

Death.

I LEAP.

My paws find purchase on a middle shelf, and I scrabble my way up, occasionally shredding a paperback spine as I scramble for a foothold. As I reach the top, the shelf teeters, then topples. Books and knickknacks cascade out. I catapult clear as the shelf lands with a crash. The box breaks open and goes tumbling, its contents spilling out across the floor. Quickly, I scan the treasures. Receipts, a leather bag of rune-stones, a rusted key...

The bedroom door flies open, and as Cara rushes in with Robbi at her heels, I see a likely target. A yellowed newspaper clipping with a photo of Cara in a skimpy costume and a man in an old-fashioned black tux. I snatch it with my teeth and race between Cara's feet. She screeches and makes a grab for me, but I slip through her fingers, a sleek flash of black.

"That cat! That, that—!"

I risk a glance behind me as she sputters, apparently frozen between a desire to attend to the mess I've made and a desire to turn me into a pair of mittens.

The mess wins. As Robbi hurries to help her, I slip through the open window and drop to the ground, leaving a curtain of dangling crystals swaying behind me.

IT TOOK both of them to lift the bookshelf and prop it back against the wall. Robbi suppressed a pang of guilt as Cara rubbed a chip in the wood. What had gotten into Trouble?

She picked up *My Life as a Rat* by Joyce Carol Oates and started to stack it with John O'Donahue's *Walking in Wonder*. Hesitated. Then she held it up and said, "Does this go with fiction or with the O's?"

Cara looked at her as if she'd grown an eye in the center of her forehead. "The Oates book goes with blue. Middle of the second shelf. *Walking in Wonder* is top left. Off-white. Why don't you just hand them to me, and I'll put them where they go."

It took almost an hour to put the room to rights—at least, as much to rights as it could be. The latch on the metal lockbox was broken, and the crystal hummingbird was in four pieces. A few of the books had claw marks on the spines. Cara tossed them in the trash, where Robbi rescued them, unable to bear the thought of throwing away perfectly readable books.

As Robbi opened the door to leave, Cara said grudgingly,

"That Death card. Usually, it just means change. Some huge upheaval that leaves your life vastly different than it was before. Ultimately, it could be a good thing."

Robbi gave her a tentative smile. "That's good to know."

Cara reached around her for the knob, already beginning to pull the door closed. "I said that's what it usually means. In light of the circumstances, you might want to consider it a little more literally."

ROBBI FOUND Trouble waiting on the stoop of Laura's cottage. Tuck was nearby, wallowing in a patch of mint.

She put her hands on her hips and looked at the cat. "Okay, big guy, what was that all about?"

With a little mew, Trouble glanced down at a piece of paper under his front paws. She sat down beside him and smoothed the creases with her hand. It was a newspaper article. The headline read, "MAGICIAN'S ASSISTANT EXONERATED!" The photo beneath was of Cara and a silver-haired man in tux and a top hat. Cara, dressed in a sequined red dress that left little to the imagination, rested one hand just below the man's boutonniere. The story opened with an alliterative teaser: "Femme Fatale or Va-va-victim?"

Robbi skimmed the story, then read aloud to Trouble and Tuck. "When stage magician Rupert ("The Great") Fallini hired sexy knife-thrower Cara Ashkali, he might have intended to spice up his show with a pulse-pounding combination of beauty and danger. What he probably didn't intend was to wind up in the morgue, a victim of a trick gone wrong."

According to the article, Fallini's show involved a series of increasingly difficult magic tricks, followed by a demonstration of Fallini's knife-throwing skill. With Cara strapped to a spinning wheel, the Great Fallini threw a dozen knives at the spaces around her, getting as close as possible without hitting her. Audiences loved it. The twist came at the end, when the two of them switched places.

But the final twist came the day Cara missed.

The question was, had she? Or had she hit exactly what she'd intended?

CHAPTER TWELVE

They hold Laura's funeral in the nearby Baptist chapel a few days later. The little church is filled with flowers, and Laura's friends pour in from across the country, most dressed in historical costume, just the way Laura would have wanted it. They squeeze in elbow to elbow in the wooden pews, and when the pews are full, they stand along the walls. It seems Elinore was wrong when she said Laura hadn't many friends. I slip inside early and take a spot in the choir loft. My inescapable shadow, by which I mean Tuck, follows.

I'm not sure if I'm growing fond of him, or if he's simply worn me down.

Robbi gives the eulogy. At first, I'm afraid she won't get through it, but somehow she does, smiling through tears as she paints a portrait of Laura and their friendship. By the time Dale takes his mandolin to the front and sings "Touch of a Phoenix," the audience is audibly sobbing. With a mournful oink, Tuck lays his head on his front hooves. I pride myself on my emotional detachment and objectivity, but even I feel a bit gutted.

Mal steps up to the podium and recites from memory a Henry Van Dyke poem that he says was Laura's favorite.

"Time is

Too Slow for those who Wait,

Too Swift for those who Fear,

Too Long for those who Grieve,

Too Short for those who Rejoice,

But for those who Love,

Time is not."

He pauses for a moment, as if he wants to add something more. Then he lays one hand over his heart and gestures with the other toward Laura's polished cherry wood coffin. "We'll miss you," he says, and then the service is over.

I only knew Laura for a week, but this is an emotional moment. Perhaps because I genuinely liked her, perhaps because I knew the future she hoped for and would never have, perhaps only because her red hair and bookish nature remind me of Tammy. It takes two of Miller's kidney pastries before I feel restored to my former state of equanimity. Tuck, being a pig, requires five.

It's another full week before they hold the competition. The three contestants spend most of their days practicing, and in his spare time Guy promotes the contest to every town less than three hours from Sherwood. Radio appearances, banner ads on the sites of local businesses, flyers on community bulletin boards. Special performance! Discount Prices!

I make myself useful keeping an eye on the suspects and encouraging Robbi during her training sessions.

Unfortunately, I unearth no more secrets. Fortunately, no one else dies.

. . .

THE MORNING OF THE TOURNAMENT, Mal woke up before dawn, too anxious to sleep. There was a lot at stake. His home, this life, even what little money he and Elinore might have gotten from whatever deal Guy hoped to arrange. Mal knew he should have talked with his sister before making his wager, but he'd been too angry to think that far ahead.

She hadn't called him on it, had even backed his play.

He hoped he would prove worthy of her trust.

Muffling a groan, he pushed himself out of bed and reached for his clothes. His muscles were still sore from yesterday's sparring session on the tourney field with Guy, but he'd given as good as he got, so Guy was probably no better off. Elinore had questioned training with his competition, but the truth was, much as he would have liked to strangle Guy for his disastrous financial decisions, he and Guy needed each other. Of all his possible opponents, only Guy was good enough at swordplay to push Mal to the edge.

The flip side was that he was doing the same for Guy.

The smell of bacon and chicory coffee told him Elinore was up and making breakfast. Quickly, he pulled on boxer briefs with a Nutty Buddy protection cup, followed by knee and elbow pads under black breeches and a deep blue swordsman's shirt.

Elinore looked up when he came in. Her gray peasant dress was belted with a loose chain girdle, and she'd draped her black cloak, edged with silver, across the back of her chair. With a worried smile, she set a mug of coffee and a plate in front of him. Bacon, eggs, banana, yogurt. Breakfast of champions. He'd forgotten how nice it was to start the day with her; so many mornings lately, he was out early with Scarlett, or Elinore was off somewhere with tools and a blowtorch, working on her sculpture project.

She brought her own plate and sat down across from him. "Are you worried?"

"No point in being worried at this stage of the game." He took a bite of bacon. Just the right amount of crispness. He took a moment to savor its perfection.

"People do a lot of things there's no point in." She stirred a splash of cream into her coffee. "You and Guy know each other's weaknesses. Have you watched *her* train?"

He had. Watching Robbi fight was like watching martial ballet. He lifted his cup to his lips to hide his smile. Martial ballet as practiced by a mongoose. Small and quick, with an instinctive grace. But a mongoose was only a threat if you were a mouse or a cobra. He and Guy had height, weight, and reach in their favor. "I'm more worried about Guy," he said. "At least in the first round."

"And I'm worried about you. Every time you look at her, you get all gooey-eyed. I don't want you to get hurt again."

"No worries on that count. She showed her colors when she shoehorned her way into this."

But had she? The thought nagged at him like a pebble in his shoe. Didn't she have every right to be a part of this? Both as a shareholder and as Laura's friend? Once the stakes had been established, could he really blame her for wanting to weigh in? Maybe he was being a jerk by not giving her the benefit of the doubt.

"Stop that," Elinore said, but she smiled when she said it. "There you go, thinking again."

He returned her grin. "Guilty as charged."

"You're a good man. You want to believe everyone else is

good too." She drained her cup and got up to refill it. "And who knows? Maybe she is. But Robbi Bryan has no ties to our faire, no reason not to throw in with Guy and get whatever she can out of the deal. That it would leave the rest of us broke and homeless isn't her concern. Nor, I suppose, should it be."

"Homeless, yes," he said. "But not exactly broke. We have some savings, and, if she sells, some of us would still get something for our shares."

"Joanne," Elinore said. "She's the only one who hasn't sold or wagered hers."

The enormity of his responsibility was like a punch to the gut. He'd known, of course. He just hadn't stopped to think about the implications. If he won, they could all keep their homes and redistribute the shares equitably again before worrying about how to save Guy from his creditors.

But if he didn't win...

He suppressed a wave of resentment. This would never have become an issue if Laura had sold him the shares she'd promised. Instead, she'd put it off, made one excuse after another, until it was too late. Sometimes he thought she'd never intended to sell them in the first place. That she'd used him as a shield until she had Dale, then intentionally reneged on their agreement.

He didn't want to think those things, because they were a betrayal of his friendship with Laura and she wasn't here to defend herself. In fact, if he were honest with himself, he had to concede that part of his anger at Robbi could be displaced anger over other betrayals in his life. And if that was true, he owed her an apology.

He looked down at his empty plate. How had that happened?

"Still thinking," Elinore teased, as if reading his mind.

He carried his plate and mug to the sink. "Can I help you clean up?"

She waved him toward his room. "You should finish getting ready. Get your head in the right place. Because whatever happens, today is going to be intense."

While she washed the breakfast dishes, he went back to his room, put on a padded gambeson, then shimmied into his chainmail shirt. He strapped on his scabbard and sheathed his rattan sword, then picked up his shield and tucked his helmet under his arm. The latter was a gift from Elinore, a gorgeous bascinet-style helmet polished to a shine and attached to a chainmail aventail designed to protect his neck and shoulders. He loved it, but it was hot. And heavy. He'd wait to put it on until it was time to fight.

Not for the first time, he imagined what his ex would say if she could see him now. *Playing Prince Valiant*, she'd say, her lip curling upward in her signature sneer. *Or is it Prince Charming?*

He stepped out, shaking his head as if her memory were an Etch-a-Sketch drawing he could erase from his life.

ROBBI STOOD beside Trouble at the edge of the tournament field, watching as the crowd trickled in. The vendors were already setting up, and the smell of turkey legs and Belgian waffles filled the air. Her stomach fluttered. How had she gotten herself into this?

She bent one leg and pulled it up behind her, stretching the muscle. Then she repeated the move on the other side before closing her eyes and taking a few deep breaths. Calming her mind, like her *sifu* had taught her.

"Are you sure you want to do this?" Guy came up beside her wearing a black gambeson under the most stunning cuirass Robbi had ever seen. It was rich, dark leather, accented at the sides with strips of black leather studded with steel. In the center of his chest was a Celtic cross, a steel stud at each tip. With pauldrons to protect his shoulders and hinged segments below the breastplate for mobility, the armor looked as functional as it was beautiful.

She felt dowdy by comparison, her hockey pads and carpet-and-duct-tape armor hidden by a tunic and a tabard, belted at the waist. But it wasn't the shine on the armor that mattered. It was the skill and focus underneath. "Are you?"

With a rueful laugh, he said, "Considering my fortune, my faire, and my life are at stake here? What choice do I have?"

Robbi was grateful when Cara, in a royal blue French Renaissance gown, strolled over and tucked her arm into Guy's. "I have something to give you," she murmured, just loud enough for Robbi to hear. "For luck."

Cara hadn't said much to Robbi since the reading, which was something of a blessing. The day after Trouble had shown her the article, Robbi had done a search for the unfortunate magician's autopsy report. There was nothing enlightening there. The man had bled to death from a wound to the neck, but given the dangerous nature of what was known in the entertainment business as impalement arts, it was impossible to tell whether the wound had been delivered accidentally or on purpose.

A little more digging, and Robbi found an ex-wife and a daughter, both of whom were eager to share their suspicions. Cara, they said, had been trying to worm her way into his affections—and his will—from the day they met. When he finally made it clear that his interest in her was purely professional, she'd killed him.

"Before that, though," his daughter said, "she did everything she could to make him dependent on her. He got food poisoning the week before he died. I'm pretty sure she gave him some bad juice, just so she could nurse him back to health."

Watching Cara adjust Guy's studded gauntlets, Robbi thought of the sour look Cara had given her when she walked into Guy's hospital room. It was no secret Cara still carried a torch for the dashing castle laird. Was Guy's poisoning an attempt to win him back?

But if that was the case, how did Laura's death fit in?

That's enough, Robbi.

She needed to focus.

As she began a series of martial arts stretches, she saw Mal stride toward the field. He looked like he'd stepped out of an Arthurian novel, dark curls lifting in the breeze, that distracting dimple flashing as he fielded a greeting from a visitor. Then she saw Tuck trundling along behind him, snuffling at the ground as if someone might have already dropped a scrap of turkey.

The valiant knight and his noble pig. Despite her pique at Mal, she stifled a giggle.

I WATCH with interest as the three contestants draw lots to determine the order of combat. Mal and Guy are to fight first, with Robbi taking on the winner. Standing between them, she looks like a waif. If I hadn't seen the infamous martial arts flip on the bridge, I would worry for her.

There are already several hundred spectators, and the growing audience makes it difficult to keep watch on all the Rennies, all of whom are in the crowd, save for the two who are competing. Even Miller has foregone the opportunity to sell his pastries to the guests in favor of a front row seat. He sits alone on the risers, staring at the tourney field and dabbing at his forehead with a handkerchief. I feel a pang of pity for him, which I quickly quash. Just because he shares his wares with Tuck and me doesn't mean he's not a killer. Humans are complex.

A recorded fanfare sounds, and Dale, in his full bardish garb, steps onto the podium at the far end of the field. Normally, Guy would do the introductions, but he's on the sidelines, warming up with his blade.

I call it a blade. In reality, although he's done his best to make it look as real as possible, only the hilt is authentic. The rest is rattan covered in some sort of metallic tape and engraved with what appear to be Viking runes.

The rules are simple. A strike to the leg, and the "wounded" combatant kneels. A strike to the arm, and it's held behind the combatant's back. Head, neck, and torso strikes are considered fatal.

Sheriff Hammond is to serve as marshal, although I have my doubts as to his objectivity. The man is as bent as a nine-bob note. Fortunately, he's only there to catch the most egregious fouls and omissions. Mostly, strikes are decided on the honor system. If it feels like a solid hit, one is honor-bound to acknowledge it.

In the face of such large stakes, it seems a fragile system.

Dale welcomes the visitors and explains the rules of the competition. He omits the part about the wager and the fate of the faire, instead weaving a tale about three rivals vying for the king's favor. He casts Mal as a disgraced hero fighting to redeem his reputation, Guy as the rogue with a heart of gold, and Robbi as the only remaining offspring of a minor lord whose lands are in contention.

The first contest begins. Mal and Guy clasp forearms, then square off. Mal holds a sword and shield, Guy a longsword and a smaller rattan blade, a main-gauche. As soon as Hammond gives the signal, Guy feints, then ducks with a jab to Mal's left side. Mal dodges, and the blow just skims his armor. They square off again.

Around the field, the dance goes on. A jab, a feint, a slash. Guy's style is sharper, flashier. He wields his weapon like a showman, but the man is no charlatan. The audience oohs and aahs at his skill and artistry. Mal bides his time, his sword a tool in the hands of a master craftsman.

They seem evenly matched, two men who know each other's moves and strategies. Soon both are panting, drenched with sweat. Guy scores a hit to Mal's shield arm. Mal drops the shield and puts the arm behind his back. The next hit goes to Mal; Guy loses his main-gauche. It moves quickly after that. Mal takes a leg hit, then another.

Hammond asks him, "Do you yield?"

Mal shakes his head. On both knees, one hand behind his back, he raises his weapon. When Guy comes in for the kill, Mal dives beneath Guy's sword, swinging his own in a sideways arc. I can hear the "thwack!" from the sidelines as Mal connects with Guy's leather backplate.

Guy wheels, sword raised, and for a moment I think he's going to charge. Then, with a disbelieving laugh, he drops to his knees and topples forward with a flourish. A showman to the last.

Though he doesn't look happy about it, Hammond calls the match in Mal's favor. Then the two men help each other up and stagger to the sidelines for water. Cara is quick to bring a flask for Guy. Miss Scarlett, who must have arrived with Elinore, meets Mal with a concerned yip, while Tuck flops down on Mal's right foot. Mal shakes his head with an indulgent smile and reaches for the water skin Elinore is holding out. Lucky for him, Tuck is still a small pig.

I glance at Robbi, a little embarrassed that I've been too caught up in the match to keep her in my sights. She's watching Mal intently, and I realize she's taking his measure, sizing him up for weaknesses. Whatever he might have been to her before this, now he's only an opponent.

MAL TOOK a grateful swig of water from the skin his sister offered, then waved off the protein bar she tried to press into his hand.

Elinore frowned. "You need to keep your strength up."

"I'm fine."

"Mal, don't underestimate that girl. She may look like a lost kitten, but she isn't going to fight like one."

"Believe me, I'm not underestimating her."

"No? Then just do me a favor." She handed him a bar she'd made from almond butter, honey, and a variety of nuts. "Eat something anyway."

ROUND TWO. Mal seems somewhat refreshed by whatever Elinore gave him. Still, as he walks to the center of the field, his step is heavier than it was before. I hope this bodes well for Robbi. Of the three, she's by far the least experienced at swordplay, but she's been training hard this past week. Joanne has appointed herself Robbi's personal trainer, and each day after Falcor was flown and fed, the two spent hours throwing axes, sparring with wooden swords, and skewering rings for the equitation phase of the competition.

If I had fingers, I would cross them for her.

Again, the combatants clasp forearms and square off to wait for the signal. When it comes, the audience shifts forward in their seats. There's a David and Goliath feel in the air, and the excitement that dynamic generates mitigates a certain lack of drama in this match. Mal and Robbi are both thoughtful fighters, both armed with sword and shield. Neither has Guy's sense of the theatrical.

Robbi is quick, but quickness may not be enough. Despite her skills in hand-to-hand, she isn't practiced in armed combat. The shield is both heavy and cumbersome, and a week of training can't make up for Mal's years of experience. Still, she gives it her best. She darts in, takes her shot. He blocks her easily, the power of his counter-blow rocking her back. Neither scores a hit. They separate, circling, strategizing.

It's a cautious fight, and I can see he doesn't want to hurt her. Perhaps he's handicapped by chivalry. Perhaps he simply doesn't want to be the villain of this tale. Clearly, the audience is on her side.

I can also see she's tiring, unused to the weight of the armor, shield, and helm. My stomach goes a tad bit collywobbles, and I realize how much I hope she wins. I begin to pace the sidelines, tail lashing.

Robbi steps back, gives herself a moment to gather her strength, then flings aside her shield and goes in at him hard and fast, a last-ditch effort, what they call in American football a Hail Mary.

Her sword comes up beneath his shield and she tags him once above the knee. Elinore cries out, and at the sound, Mal's shoulders straighten. He goes to one knee, but before Robbi can land a second blow, Mal's blade meets hers with a force that drives her sword up and leaves her torso open. He follows with a thrust to the midsection that knocks the wind out of her and drops her to knees.

It takes her a moment to remember to die.

IGNORING MAL'S PROFFERED HAND, Robbi pushed herself to her feet and made her way unsteadily toward the sidelines, pulling off her helmet. She hadn't expected to win this one, so she was surprised at the depth of her disappointment. Had she not wanted to lose, or had she simply not wanted to lose to Mal?

Joanne met her halfway. "Are you all right?" She reached for Robbi's helm and traded it for a water bottle dripping with condensation.

Robbi downed half of it, then pressed the bottle to her forehead. It cooled her skin and made her feel mostly human again. "Aside from acute embarrassment and a bad case of hat head?"

"You handled yourself well out there," Joanne said. "I plead the Fifth about the hat head."

Robbi polished off the water, then tried to fluff her damp hair with her fingers. "At least that's over. If I can win the next two, we won't have to go to throwing axes."

"Then that's what you need to do," Joanne said. "Because I've seen you throw an axe."

Trouble was waiting for her on the sidelines. He rubbed against her legs as if commiserating. "It's okay, big guy," she said, though she didn't think she sounded completely convincing. She bent to stroke his head. "We'll get 'em this time."

While Dale and Sheriff Hammond set up the archery targets, Robbi peeled out of her armor and dropped it in the grass. Without it, she felt a hundred pounds lighter, like a helium balloon. She tipped back her head and raised her arms, appreciating the cooling effect of sweat evaporating in the breeze.

"You gave me quite a fight." Mal's voice made her jump. "Sorry if I hurt you."

Quickly, she lowered her arms. "Did you say the same to Guy?"

He laid her shield beside her armor. "I did not."

"Why not?"

"Because I wasn't sorry."

A burst of static erupted from the podium. Then Dale's voice came through the speakers, announcing the next stage of the competition. Three competitors. Three targets. Three arrows each.

Robbi glanced toward the barn, where Joanne was emerging with her bow and quiver, then looked back at Mal. "Should I say break a leg, or is that just for theater?"

Mal made a sweeping motion, taking in the crowd, the vendors, the banners rippling in the breeze. "It's theater for them," he said. "I guess that counts."

THE ARCHERY PORTION of the competition goes quickly. The three competitors line up a little more than two hundred feet in front of the targets, Robbi on the right, Mal on the left, Guy in the center.

Something cold and wet nudges my haunch, and I leap to one side, hissing. It's only Tuck's nose. Annoyed, I bat at it with my paws, and the silly knobhead plops back onto his haunches with a startled grunt. I give a low growl to let him know he's lucky I didn't use my claws.

Mal goes first. He takes his time and gets off three good shots. The first one hits just inside the yellow bullseye. The other two both touch the center x, which Robbi says is called the spider.

Guy steps up next. His arrows make a tight triangle, each one touching a leg of the x. He grins. It's a better cluster than Mal's.

Robbi's turn. She pulls an arrow from her quiver and nocks it. It's a work of art, a gorgeous handmade arrow carved from Norway pine and fletched with turkey feathers, then lovingly oiled and sanded to a silky finish. She draws the bow and anchors the string, index finger at the corner of her mouth, top finger under her cheekbone, thumb under the jaw.

The arrow flies straight and true, striking between two legs of the x. Her second thuds into the center of the spider. She takes a breath and lines up her third shot. I watch it sail toward the target. It splits the second arrow with a crack and drives it through the center of the paper target in a feat of skill known in the archery world as a Robin Hood.

I'm so excited that before I can stop myself, I let out a chirp and dig my claws into the nearest leg. Joanne gives a little screech and, embarrassed, I disengage before she can shake me off. I sit with my back to her, pretending to groom myself.

When I look up again, Guy is staring at the split arrow in shock and dismay. Mal's jaw is set, a picture of determination.

This puts the tally at one match for Robbi, one for Mal. If Guy wins equitation, it will be a three-way tie, and they'll pull out the throwing axes. Otherwise, either Robbi or Mal takes it all.

While the archers pull their arrows from the targets, and Joanne goes inside the barn to prepare the horses for the next phase of the competition, Dale announces an hour-long break. The crowd divides, some converging on the food wagons, others heading for the lavatories, which I've heard the British sometimes call the House of Lords. I find that smashing, so much better than the vulgar "loo" or "toilet."

In all the chaos, it will be impossible to keep track of all the Rennies. As I glance around for a likely target, Guy disengages from Cara and strolls toward the far side of the field with Sheriff Hammond. My decision is made.

I follow them, and Tuck follows me. If I were human, I would worry about arousing their suspicion, but I know they won't think twice about our presence. Humans always underestimate animals.

I know Guy has mucked everything up, but I feel more than a little sorry for him. No matter how this ends, someone is going to be hurt. It's my job to make sure it isn't Robbi.

WHILE THE RIDERS saddled and bridled their horses, Joanne and Dale set up the ring-jousting course. It consisted of a series of poles of varying heights, each with a two-inch ring loosely attached to the top. Each rider had eight seconds to run the course, spearing each ring with a foam and cardboard lance. The one with the most rings would win the round. In the event of a tie, there would be a second run, with the size of the rings decreased by a quarter inch. A rider who finished outside the eight-second limit would be disqualified.

Robbi half-listened as Dale explained the rules to the audience. The rest of her mind focused on the ride ahead. Joanne had lent Robbi her Friesian, Freyja, and in some ways, it was a good match. The black mare was as close to bombproof as a horse could be, with the perfect blend of common sense and spirit. From a size perspective, it was a different matter. The first day Robbi rode her, she felt like a toddler on a mechanical bull. She couldn't grip with her legs. She couldn't give the right aids. All she could do was perch on top and hang on.

She and Joanne had spent the entire next day driving to every tack shop and farm supply store in the area before they found a second-hand saddle large enough for Freyja with a small enough seat for Robbi. Riding the big mare was still a challenge, but Robbi thought she'd learned to compensate. And she had a good eye, an archer's eye. She thought she had a chance.

Guy rode first, his horse a pale dun Lusitano he called Galileo. He stroked the gelding's neck and murmured something in its ear. Then he lowered his lance and urged the horse into a gallop. At the end of the course, he held up his lance and rode a lap around the field, flirting with the audience, wowing the crowd. He'd captured every ring.

Mal rode next. Robbi had pegged Guy as the man to beat, but Mal rode like he was half centaur, his Andalusian stallion responding to cues Robbi couldn't even see. At the end of the ride, he shifted his weight backward, and the horse pulled to a stop as Mal held up his lance. Another perfect score.

"Okay, girl." Robbi reached down and rubbed the mare's sleek neck. This had to be a perfect ride. "Let's show them how it's done." She lowered the lance, and the mare surged forward. One ring. She dipped the lance to scoop up a ring from a lower pole, then tipped it up to snatch a higher one. Four rings...then five. The rings, which had seemed so small before, had grown huge in her focus, and at the end of the ride, she too had made a perfect run.

Round two, another tie. Round three, the rings were half an inch smaller. Robbi and the two men exchanged glances, looked at the tips of their lances. Sooner or later, one of them was going to miss.

Guy started forward, lance down, riding hard, feet pressing in the stirrups. A moment later, he lurched to one side and, with a startled shout, tumbled off the horse. He cried out again as he hit the ground, one leg bent at an impossible angle.

Galileo jogged to a stop, one stirrup leather ragged and empty.

A startled buzz ran through the audience. Then, as Cara flew across the field, one hand holding up the skirt of her gown, a voice came from the back of the crowd. "I'm a doctor. Let me through!"

WHILE THE SHERIFF tries to maintain order, a woman's voice cries out from inside the barn. Robbi has gone to secure Guy's horse, so Mal is closest. I streak across the field, arriving at the barn just behind him. Somewhere behind me, I hear Tuck wheezing as he tries and fails to keep up.

At first, nothing seems amiss, but a quick peek into the back aisle reveals the body of a cloaked and hooded woman crumpled on the floor, an arrow jutting from her back.

I give a yowl and Mal comes running. Kneeling beside the woman, he pulls back the hood of her cloak to reveal dark curls and a face pale with pain.

Elinore.

She gives a little moan, and Mal lets out a relieved breath. She's alive.

I move to get a closer look at the arrow. It's a gorgeous, handmade wooden arrow made from Norway pine.

One of Robbi's.

CHAPTER THIRTEEN

In the waiting area of Sherwood Medical Center's emergency room, Mal paced an arc from the sliding glass doors to the vending machines and back. He felt fourteen again, waiting to see if his mother would survive her latest episode of "nerves." He'd been helpless against an enemy he could neither see nor touch, forced to trust strangers with the life of someone he loved. He could only hope his sister's physical wounds would prove more treatable than the fractures in their mother's psyche.

"She's going to be okay," Joanne said. She looked cramped and uncomfortable, squeezed into an ugly plastic chair. With a glance toward Cara she added, "Guy too."

Cara nodded absently, her gaze creeping from the e-book on her cell phone to the doors between them and the treatment rooms. Mal knew how she felt. Each tick of the second hand felt like an hour.

They were the only people in the waiting area, except for a buxom woman behind the desk. Her raised eyebrows on their arrival were the only indication that a group of grown people in medieval garb was any less common than a working man in overalls. Just a normal day in the ER. Small town or no, she'd probably seen her share of strangeness.

Cara shifted in her seat. "What's taking them so long?"

"X-rays," Mal said. "Maybe surgery. We don't know how bad Guy's break was, or how much damage the arrow did to Elinore."

"Robbi's arrow," Cara reminded him. As if he could forget.

Joanne bristled. "Anybody could have gotten one of Robbi's arrows. Her quiver was hanging in the barn all morning. Robbi wouldn't hurt Elinore any more than I would have hurt Guy."

Cara's eyes slitted. "We still don't know you didn't."

Mal stopped in mid-pace. "We all know Joanne would never hurt Guy. But what do we know about Robbi?"

"We know she loved Laura," Joanne said softly, "and that Laura loved her. We know she's not stupid. Why would she use her own arrow?"

Mal rubbed his temples. Why indeed? Convenience? A message of some kind?

Cara rolled her eyes. "Killers use their own weapons all the time. Mostly, that's how they get caught."

"Sure," Joanne agreed. "But they rarely leave weapons with their names on them at the crime scene."

Slowly, Mal nodded. An arrow as distinctive as the one that had struck Elinore might as well have had Robbi's signature on it.

Cara wasn't ready to give in. "She might have, if she was trying to make a point."

"What point?" Joanne asked. "To whom? And all that aside,

do you think she'd incriminate herself in a crime against Mal's sister?"

Cara hesitated. Then, she said grudgingly, "You make a good case."

Mal looked from one to the other. "What case? What difference does it make whose sister El is?"

Joanne's ears turned red. "Don't tell me you haven't noticed."

"Noticed what? Robbi and I haven't spoken in a week."

Cara gave a little snort of laughter. "For a smart man, Mal, you're pretty slow."

He blew out an exasperated breath. "Just drop it, okay? With any luck, Elinore can tell us what happened."

As if on cue, the door to the treatment area swung open, and a striking woman in scrubs pushed Elinore out in a wheelchair. Mal hurried over and knelt beside her. "How are you feeling?"

"I'm fine," El said, but he didn't think she looked fine.

The woman in scrubs gestured toward her name badge. "I'm Dr. Van Owen. And you are?"

"Mal McClaren. Her brother."

The doctor nodded. "Your sister is a very lucky woman. It was a shallow wound, not much blood loss. In fact, it's likely she was stabbed with the arrow, rather than shot. I put in a few stitches and covered it with antibacterial ointment. Gave her a tetanus shot. Just keep an eye on it, make sure there's no infection." She handed him a small rectangle of paper. "Antibiotics and something for pain."

Mal tried to pay attention to her instructions, but his mind kept pulling him back to the question of his sister's attacker. The window of time during which it could have happened was fairly small, but with the crowd milling about, almost everyone was unaccounted for at some point.

The doctor's voice cut through his trance. "Mr. McClaren?"

"Sorry. Got it. I'll get these filled on the way home."

The door swung open again, and a pretty young nurse pushed Guy out in another wheelchair. His leg, in an electric blue cast, was elevated on one leg rest. "Broken in three places," he said. Holding up his crutches, he added, "Guess I won't be riding in round four."

Mal didn't answer. What was he supposed to say? It's okay, Guy. We'll reschedule for eight weeks from now, when you're back on your feet?

It wasn't okay.

In the awkward silence, Cara swiped her e-reader app closed and tucked her phone into her purse. "We can worry about that later," she said. "I'm sure there will be a do-over."

Guy shook his head. "No do-overs," he said. "I've ruined everything. I deserve to lose the faire."

THE CELL SEEMED TINIER from inside than it had from the other side of the bars. Robbi sat cross-legged on the single cot and tried without luck to meditate. Her monkey mind was all over the place, mostly regaling her with dire predictions of her death in the electric chair. It just went to show you couldn't depend on yourself to be rational under duress. As far as she knew, Tennessee had never electrocuted a woman.

That didn't mean she wasn't in big trouble.

She replayed the morning's events in her mind. The armored combat, in which she'd failed so spectacularly. Her third arrow flying so straight and true it felt like angels had been guiding it. Waiting her turn before the ring joust, Freyja's bridle in her hand, her head turning to soak in the sweet smell of the mare's neck. There had been time, not much time, between Joanne bringing out the horses and the discovery of the semi-conscious Elinore. That narrow time frame meant attacking Elinore was a huge risk. Why choose that moment, and that weapon, when there were so many other times and places that would have been easier?

Then there had been that other window of time, the one between Joanne's inspection of the saddles and Guy's accident. Because it hadn't really been an accident, had it? When Robbi had caught Galileo, she had examined the broken end of the stirrup leather. Its inside facing had been nearly cut through, leaving a strap that, from the outside, looked completely normal, even as Guy's weight stressed the weakened leather until it snapped.

That level of risk-taking spoke of desperation—or obsession. As far as she could tell, though, that didn't eliminate anyone.

A traitorous little voice inside her head whispered, *Joanne had the most opportunity*.

It made her feel sick to think about it, after everything the big woman had done to help her prepare for the competition. Driving from tack store to tack store, sparring with their rattan swords, sharing confidences over a glass of wine or mead after a long, hard day of training...it had felt like friendship. Robbi hoped she could trust it.

Footsteps sounded in the hall outside her cell. Sheriff Hammond strolled over to the bars and stared in at her, hands in his pockets. "Too bad you didn't listen to that good advice I gave the other day."

Robbi laughed. "Because if I had, you could have strong-armed Guy into selling the faire?"

He hitched his belt up over his belly. "Guy doesn't need me to strong-arm him. He's got some nasty creditors from Vegas to do that. Me, I just want him to cut his losses and get out alive."

"More good advice?"

He smirked. "What can I say? I'm a sage at heart."

She crossed her arms. "Don't flatter yourself. You're just a dirty cop."

"Dirty cop?" He leaned forward, perhaps trying to invade her space, the way he had when they'd met in the hospital parking lot.

With the bars between them, it lost much of its menace, and she had to remind herself that he held all the power in this situation. It was stupid to antagonize him.

Hammond said, "You know how much I get paid to deal with a bunch of Uncle Leroys who think they can make a better living selling meth than moonshine? To tell some poor farm boy's mom her kid got crushed racing tractors over on Haint Holler? I'll tell you what I get paid. Not enough."

He stepped back, breathing heavily. After a moment, he added, "Anyway, it's not illegal for me to buy shares in a private business."

"Then why have you been trying so hard to hide it?"

His eyes grew small and mean. "Little girl," he said. "You shoulda gone back home when you still had the chance."

I'M WAITING in the truck bed when they return. I've finally had time to think back to the conversation I overheard at the tournament, when

I followed Guy and Hammond. It provided no new information, but it did confirm our suspicions that the sheriff is Guy's silent partner. "You owe me," Hammond said. "I want that sale to go through yesterday."

"It's not that simple," Guy protested, but Hammond cut him off.

"Make it that simple," he said, and stalked away.

I'm not sure yet what I can do with that confirmation, but I'm beginning to form a plan.

While I'm thinking it over, Mal pushes his sister's wheelchair across the parking lot to the truck. Joanne trundles behind, pushing Guy's. Mal raises an eyebrow when he sees me. Then, with an amused smile, he shakes his head. Joanne laughs out loud, then helps Guy into the back seat and closes the door behind him.

"Can we ask now?" Cara says, sliding in the opposite door and scooting to the middle so she can sit beside Guy. "Elinore, what happened?"

Unfortunately, Elinore has no idea. "I was looking for Tuck," she says, as Mal helps her from the wheelchair into the passenger seat of his truck, "and I thought he might be getting into Joanne's feed again."

Joanne thumps a fist into the opposite palm. "That little scoundrel!"

"No," Elinore says. "Not this time. He wasn't in the feed room, so I went into the back aisle, and that's when I felt this awful pain under my shoulder blade. Like I'd been stabbed with a hot poker. The next thing I remember is Mal kneeling beside me. I must have passed out from the pain."

Mal says, "So you didn't see who did it. Did you hear a voice? Did they say anything?"

"Not that I remember."

"What about a smell?" Joanne asks. "You know, like aftershave or perfume?"

"Deputy Debba asked me that too, but no, nothing. Not that I recall."

Carefully, Mal tucks Elinore's skirt under her legs to keep the door from catching it. "We'll talk about it later. After you get some rest."

Joanne crosses to the passenger side, then hesitates. "What about Robbi?"

Wincing, Elinore turns her head and says over her shoulder, "What about her?"

"We can't just leave her there with Hammond. If he really is Guy's silent partner, who knows what he'll do to her?"

Elinore doesn't seem surprised at the accusation, so I assume Mal has kept her up to date. "Based on what I've seen, she's pretty good at taking care of herself."

Cara leans forward. "Do you think she's the one who shot you?"

"She doesn't remember," Joanne snaps, as I nimbly leap from the truck bed and slip into the back seat floorboard. "But whoever did it, it wasn't Robbi. And Elinore was stabbed, not shot. Don't you remember what the doctor said?"

Cara plops back against the back seat with enough force to make Guy wince. Then she scowls at me and says, "I can't help it. I don't trust her."

I meet her gaze with an aplomb that would make Double-O-Seven proud. I suspect she's realized that the article from her lockbox is missing; naturally, she blames Robbi for its disappearance.

"I do," Joanne says, and slams the door to punctuate the affirmation. "Mal, you do too, don't you?"

For a moment, he's silent. From my spot on the floorboard, I imagine him resting his hands on the steering wheel, weighing the evidence in his mind. "I want to," he says at last, then adds, "We'll come back for her, after we get these two back home."

He doesn't, though, partly because he doesn't want to leave Elinore alone so soon, and partly because the arraignment won't be held until the next afternoon. Instead, he gives Joanne his bank card and PIN number to cover half of Robbi's bail, and she drives back to Sherwood the next day with me riding shotgun.

After a foiled attempt to slip past courthouse security, I'm forced to wait in the car while Joanne goes inside to try and convince a judge to set bail over Sheriff Hammond's objections.

I'm sure she's going to be splendid. All the same, I wish I could be there. Everyone knows black cats are good luck.

THE JUDGE'S gavel struck the block, and without a word to the gallery, he gathered up his robes and strode from the bench. As he disappeared into his chambers, Robbi turned to Joanne, who sat beside her at the plaintiff's table in a black-skirted power suit half a size too small. Robbi flung her arms around the bigger woman. "Joanne, you were brilliant!"

Joanne extricated herself from the embrace. Her cheeks were pink, but she was grinning. "I did do pretty good, didn't I? Guess the old girl hasn't forgotten all her courtroom tricks."

Laughing with relief, Robbi remembered the image her mind had conjured when she'd first heard about Joanne's former profession: a corporate Amazon in a power suit and wolf pelt. The metaphor was apt. Somehow, against the sheriff's objections, Joanne had managed to convince the judge to set bail. She knew she wasn't out of the woods yet—a charge of Aggravated Assault was a serious thing—but at least she had a chance to find the real culprit and clear her name.

"I was worried for a while there," Joanne said, still beaming from her success. She tugged at her jacket. "It's hard to find a suit my size in a town like Sherwood, but I got rid of all my lawyer clothes when I ran off with the Rennies."

"You were perfect," Robbi said. "Better than perfect."

She suppressed the stab of guilt at her earlier suspicions. Joanne was a true friend, truer than Robbi deserved.

As they left the courtroom, Sheriff Hammond shot them a sour look. Robbi resisted the urge to respond in kind. Instead, she gave him her sweetest smile and wiggled her fingers at him in a little wave.

"You'd better keep clear of that one," Joanne said. "He doesn't seem to like you much."

"You either, now. Did I mention you were brilliant?"

"You might have. Just in passing. Maybe you should say it again, just in case."

"Brilliant, brilliant, brilliant," Robbi sing-songed. "I think we should get it put on a T-shirt."

Joanne snorted, but her victory grin broadened. "A billboard would be better."

RIDING BACK to the faire with Trouble purring on her lap, Robbi told Joanne what she'd noticed about Guy's stirrup. Joanne frowned. "So, there were two murder attempts today. Our killer's getting either brave or desperate."

"I can see wanting to kill Guy," Robbi said. "I mean, if you're the killing kind. He's the one who put the faire at risk. But why Elinore?"

Joanne grunted as her car jounced into a rut. "Maybe he thought she saw him tampering with Guy's stirrup."

"Or her. I guess so."

"Or he...she, they, it—can we just say he?—thought Elinore was onto him. There's no sign that she was, though. She doesn't have any idea who stabbed her. By the way..." She gave Robbi a sidelong glance.

"By the way, what?"

"The arrow she was stabbed with...did you get a look at it?"

Robbi shook her head. "But the sheriff told me it was one of mine. I should have counted them, I guess, but I was so focused on the competition I didn't think of it."

"We all were." Joanne pulled onto the vendors' track and then onto the Loop. Just past Dale's cottage, she lifted her foot off the gas. "Hold on. What's that?"

The door of Laura's cottage was standing open. Before the wheels stopped turning, Robbi was out of the car, with Trouble in her arms. As she set him on the grass and ran for the door, she heard Joanne's car crunch to a stop. The driver's door slammed, and Joanne's footsteps pounded up the path behind her.

Robbi dashed inside. A quick glance showed nothing out of place, but the door to Laura's bedroom was also open. Ignoring the little voice that said confronting a possibly-armed intruder might be a bad idea, she plunged into the room just as a pair of brown leather boots disappeared through the open window.

"Out the back!" she shouted to Joanne. "Cut him off!" She slithered out the window and launched herself after the figure bolting for the woods.

A streak of black passed on her right. Just as the intruder reached the tree line, the streak veered left, between the intruder's legs. The little man stumbled and fell, his brown hood falling back to reveal Miller's bald head.

Miller. That little weasel.

He scrambled to find his feet, but Trouble wove around and between them until Robbi could clap a hand on the baker's shoulder.

Joanne jogged up, panting. Her black pumps were in one

hand, and the buttons on her jacket had popped off. "Well, well." She plucked a crumpled wad of papers from Miller's shirt pocket. "What have we here?"

"N...nothing." He tried without success to squirm out of Robbi's grip. "L...l...let me go!"

Joanne held up the papers. They were all recipes, written in Laura's careful cursive. Robbi recognized one from their childhood: Chef Boyardee Chicken and Dumpling Pizza Muffins. Why in Heaven's name would Miller take that one? She and Laura had loved it, but it was a silly kids' dish, assembled from odds and ends in Aunt Esther's cabinet.

At the thought of Miller rummaging through Laura's things, Robbi spun the little man around and shook him. "Is this what you killed her for? A bunch of recipes?"

"No, no! I didn't!" Miller's face flooded with red. "I never k...killed her. I just wanted what w...was mine!"

"Her bread-and-butter-pudding recipe?" Joanne fanned the papers in front of him. "It isn't even here."

"I couldn't f...find it. When I heard your car, I just g... grabbed some instead. I didn't even look at the t...titles." Tears wobbled on his lashes.

Robbi couldn't even bring herself to feel sorry for him. "I don't believe you. Did you take her journal after you killed her?"

"J...journal?" His eyes cut from Robbi to Joanne but Robbi knew he found no sympathy in either. Even Trouble's green-gold eyes looked accusing. "I don't know what you're t...talking about."

Joanne stuffed the papers into her waistband and shoved her face closer to his. "Her journal, you little pervert. Just admit it! You couldn't stand to be rejected, so you killed her, and then you took her journal as some sick souvenir."

Robbi hadn't thought it was possible for Miller to turn any redder, but somehow he did. "I n...never liked Laura that way," he said, with surprising fervor. "I never did! Anyway, h...how do we know it wasn't you? Everybody knows you w...w...wanted Mal."

The pain in Joanne's face said he was right. Then she let out a bellow like a wounded bull and threw a punch that knocked the little baker sideways, out of Robbi's grasp. He lay on his back in the grass, blinking up at the sky, his arms splayed out like a crucifix.

For the second time that day, Robbi threw her arms around Joanne, this time to keep her from pummeling the incapacitated man. It was like trying to hold back a falling wall, but somehow she did it. Maybe Joanne was letting her.

"Laura was my friend!" Joanne sobbed into Miller's stricken face. "And why would I wait until they'd broken up if I was going to kill her? And why would I hurt Elinore?"

Slowly, the glaze faded from Miller's eyes. He pushed himself up with his elbows and scooted away on his bottom, muttering under his breath, "Hell h...hath no fury like a w...w... woman scorned."

Robbi felt Joanne's muscles bunch. "Joanne, don't. You'll kill him."

"I don't care."

Miller scooted a little farther. Trouble gave a little *mrrryeaow* as if to warn him against any more funny business.

Robbi said, "We don't even know he killed her. All we know is that he stole some recipes." She looked over at Miller. "The day Laura died. Were you in her cottage?"

"I d...didn't d...damage anything. That was the sh...sheriff's men." He lowered his head. "And you and M...Mal came back before I could f...f...find the p...pudding recipe."

He lapsed into silence. Time ticked on.

Then Joanne heaved a heavy sigh. "Okay. Okay. What are we going to do with him?"

"We can't call Hammond," Robbi said. "We don't have proof of anything except stealing a couple of recipes. And after today, the sheriff's as likely to arrest us as Miller."

"And I suppose we really can't kill him."

"Certainly not."

Another sigh. "And if we lock him up somewhere, that's kidnapping. We're just going to let him go?"

"I think we have to." Robbi looked down at Miller, trying to sort out her feelings. When she'd seen him fleeing Laura's cottage, she was certain he was the killer. Now she wasn't sure. She wagged a finger at him. "Everyone is going to know you broke into Laura's house. We're all going to be watching you."

"You're all already w...watching me," he said bitterly. "What's so d...different about that?"

By the time she'd pulled him to his feet and sent him trudging through the woods back toward the mill, Joanne had composed herself. "Sorry," she said. Then, "Look, what he said about Mal—"

"Don't worry about it," Robbi interrupted. "He doesn't know what he's talking about."

"No, he does. I told myself I'd done a good job of hiding it, but..." Joanne's broad shoulders hunched. "What I'm trying to say is, I know he doesn't like me that way. I'm okay that you like him."

"I don't like Mal," Robbi said. "Not even a little."

Not anymore. Although he had been nice today. Almost sweet, like before the competition.

Of course, that was before she was arrested for stabbing his sister.

But if he believed she'd done it surely he wouldn't have paid half her bail.

Joanne waved a dismissive hand. "Whatever you say. I know you don't need my permission, but I'm giving it to you anyway. You know, so if you change your mind, you don't feel bad about it." With a strained smile, she turned and strode away barefoot, looking almost as dejected as Miller had.

Robbi watched her go, then slowly headed back inside. She'd feed Falcor and then pour a glass of wine. Maybe read a little before she climbed into the workroom cot and tried to get some sleep. She wished Laura had been there for the tournament. She would have laughed at Guy's dramatic defeat and consoled Robbi after her loss to Mal. Robbi could almost hear her friend's cheers for her first ever Robin Hood.

Then, with a little stab of sorrow, she realized that, except for Miller's brief interrogation, this was the first time she'd thought of Laura since the tournament began.

CHAPTER FOURTEEN

Poor Robbi seems positively knackered. She says she's too tired to be hungry, but as a reward for my heroic actions in capturing and detaining Miller, she sautés several butterfly shrimp in butter for my supper. After I've eaten, I sit in front of the door and meow until she lets me out. I can tell she doesn't like the idea, but by now she seems to know that I'm both trustworthy and exceptionally capable. More important, she must know that, as the Star Trek aficionados say, "Resistance is futile." Trouble, the famous black cat detective, always finds a way.

I stop at the McClaren cottage to pick up Tuck. He seems both surprised and pleased to be included, but reluctant to leave Elinore, a sentiment with which I sympathize. Eventually, though, my exemplary powers of persuasion win him over.

I'm not certain I'll need him, but I'm not sure I won't. As some sage once said, better to have and not need than need and not have. Perhaps it was Yoda.

He trots along beside me, his cheery demeanor only slightly damp-

ened by the events of the day. It's a long walk into town, though, and by the time we reach a little grocery store a few miles down the road, he's beginning to grumble. Worse, he's slowing me down. I'm beginning to remember why I don't believe in sidekicks.

If only I were taller and had opposable thumbs, I would be able to drive. Since I can't, I scout the parking lot until I recognize a truck I've seen in town. I can easily hop into the bed, but Tuck, with his short legs, is unable to duplicate my maneuver. I glance around. We need to act quickly, before someone comes out and spots us. There is a piece of plywood in the bed, but it's too heavy for a svelte feline like myself. There's nothing of use in the toolbox. The big blue tarp will offer us a hiding place, but even if I could push it over the edge, even the nimblest of pigs is not built for climbing.

Then, a few spaces away, I see the answer. An abandoned cart. Under my expert supervision, Tuck noses it to the rear of the truck and turns it on its side. I barely manage to turn the latch, and the tailgate falls open with a bang. Tuck clambers up the cart and into the truck bed, and we dive under the tarp just in time.

We lie there, still as catnip mice, while the owner of the truck rails against vandals and pranksters. I hear him rummaging through the tool chest and fear he'll fling back the tarp next, but he mumbles that nothing seems to be missing and slams the tailgate shut. The cart rattles away. Then the engine starts, and the truck rumbles onto the road.

When it stops and I'm satisfied the owner has gone inside, we creep out from beneath the tarp. This time, Tuck helps with the latch. The tailgate falls, and he tumbles out with a little squeal. I drop onto the driveway beside him and glance around to get my bearings. Then the porch light clicks on, and as we scurry away, I hear the owner cursing his defective tailgate.

Tuck is limping from his tumble from the truck, but he only complains a little. Fortunately, Sherwood is a small town, and we quickly find what I'm looking for: the sheriff's office with its attached jail cells.

I'm not sure yet what I'm looking for. I doubt the sheriff keeps anything incriminating in his office, but one never knows. Even Moriarty made the occasional mistake, and Hammond is no Moriarty.

Besides, I want to get a look at that arrow.

MAL STOOD on Robbi's stoop, a picnic basket in one hand, a bottle of merlot in the other. It should be easy enough to tap on the door, but for some reason he couldn't bring himself to do it. It wasn't the apology that worried him; he'd been an ass and she deserved to know he knew it. It was what might come after the apology. She might toss him out on his ear. Or she might invite him in.

Both were equally terrifying.

As a vet, before his disastrous marriage, he'd spent two years treating bears and big cats for a conservation center. It was the most exciting work of his life, but even though his patients could have killed or crippled him, he hadn't been afraid. Animals were honest, if you knew how to listen, and if you listened, there was nothing to be afraid of.

Unlike with people.

He drew in a long breath, then tucked the wine under one arm and knocked. He half-hoped she wouldn't answer, and at first, he thought he was going to get his wish. Then the door swung open, and she was looking up at him with a question in her eyes. Those incredible eyes. He held up the wine bottle. "I thought you might, uh..."

He stopped, lowered his hand. Starting with his peace offering felt wrong. "I came by to say I was a jerk to you about the competition. I'm sorry. It wasn't about you."

"It felt like it was."

"It wasn't. It was..." He trailed off, not sure how to explain it.

"Baggage?"

"Exactly," he said, relieved that she understood. "Baggage."

She crossed her arms, and the look on her face said maybe he'd been too quick to assume he was forgiven. "I have baggage too. I didn't treat you like a criminal."

"A criminal?"

"Not exactly a criminal. But a bad person."

"I don't think you're a bad person. I just, well, I just...wasn't sure at the time. I didn't know you very well."

"And now?"

"I still don't know you very well." He offered a hopeful smile. "But I'd like to."

HE HAD A CUTE SMILE. And it meant something, that he'd made a special trip just to apologize. Yeah, he had been kind of a jerk, but then he'd just found out he was about to lose his home, and when he'd come up with a solution, she'd thrown a kink into his plans. It wasn't okay, but it was sort of understandable.

She looked down at the basket. "What's in there?"

"Spaghetti with meatballs. Garlic bread. Butter, fresh, hand-churned."

"Not very medieval."

"It's what I make best. I could take it back and make you a shepherd's pie instead."

She laughed. "You want me to trade your best spaghetti for inferior shepherd's pie?"

He smiled down at her. Lord, that smile. "I didn't say it was inferior. Just slightly not best."

"No dessert?" she teased.

"Chocolate cake and bread pudding. I wasn't sure which you'd like." He held up the bottle. "And I brought wine."

"Wine and chocolate. Well, that's a good start." She stepped aside so he could pass.

I EXPLAIN my plan to Tuck. Then he ambles around to the front door, and I slip into the building through an air conditioning vent. A few moments later, I hear a loud squeal and the crash of a rubbish bin. While the deputy in charge deals with the distraction Tuck has provided, I emerge into the lobby and creep into the hallway to look for the evidence room.

There doesn't seem to be one. Perhaps the arrow is in Hammond's office.

It's easy enough to find. His name is on a brass plaque on the door. It's locked, so I nudge open the door to the gentlemen's room and, thanks to my superhuman balance and athleticism, I manage to access the crawlspace by way of the acoustic ceiling tiles. From there, it's only a few yards to Hammond's office. Before I leap down, I make sure there's a path back—chair to desk to filing cabinet to ceiling tiles. Then I drop onto the cabinet and begin my search.

If Hammond's office is any example, the life of a small-town sheriff is deadly dull. Case reports in desert-dry language, requisitions for cleaning supplies and toilet paper, budget spreadsheets, and more, and more. The man is a stickler for paperwork. In a desk drawer, I find a document confirming the transfer of five of Guy's shares, along with the terms of the contract. If Guy dies, Hammond gets half his shares, which will give him the same number as Robbi. But if Robbi dies without a will, her shares revert to Guy, and if he should die as well, Hammond will have more than enough shares to ram the sale of the faire through.

That sounds like motive to me.

Outside, I hear Tuck starting up again. Three times, that was the plan. I must hurry. I find the arrow in a cardboard evidence box beside Sheriff Hammond's desk. I lack the resources to test for fingerprints, but I do notice that the nock of the arrow, the end with the fletching, has been damaged. The wood on two sides is chipped and scratched, the feathers rumpled. Whoever stole Robbi's arrow would have been in a hurry. Perhaps they shoved it fletching-first into a bag or satchel.

The noise outside has died down, and now I hear Tuck's third distraction. The deputy sounds angrier, Tuck more frightened. Quickly I nudge the top of the evidence box back into place and make my escape. Then I hurry to the front of the building.

The deputy, armed with a catch stick and a taser, has Tuck backed into the corner where the main building meets the jail wing. Tuck shrinks back, his small eyes widening in fear.

My hackles rise.

Trouble the Vanquisher to the rescue.

LORD, the carbs. But shepherd's pie was carby too, and the spaghetti was delicious. A sliver of cake and a dollop of bread pudding topped off the meal. A very small dollop. She swallowed the last bite of her cake and took a taste of the pudding. Divine.

She lowered her spoon as a thought occurred to her. "How is Elinore? Are you sure you should have left her?"

"She's sleeping. Joanne is with her."

"This was Joanne's idea?" Robbi nodded toward the pasta, trying to suppress her disappointment. She'd been impressed by his gesture, but if someone else had put him up to it, it wasn't quite as moving.

"No, I told her I'd been planning to, but I didn't want to leave Elinore alone. Joanne said she'd stay over in case El woke up and needed anything. But she probably won't. The meds pretty much knocked her out."

"Mal, you know..." She stopped. Joanne's crush was her own secret to tell—or not tell, as the case may be. Though it didn't seem like much of a secret, since even Miller knew. Still, she switched tacks. Better to err on the side of safety. "That first day I came here, I thought Joanne might have been the killer. I mean, she did go after Tuck with an axe."

"She's all bluster and no bite. You don't still think she could have killed Laura?"

"No. Not anymore." She topped off both their glasses, then took a final bite of the bread pudding. "Shall we go finish our wine in the living room? If I stay here, that pudding is going to keep calling me."

Smooth, Robbi, smooth.

He sat on the couch, not at the end, not in the center. More like the center of the end. She wavered. Should she sit beside him? Or across from him in the recliner? And if she did sit on the couch, how close was too close? How far was too far? She wanted a friendly distance, but not too forward. She wasn't sure yet if she was interested, or if he was. But he'd brought her dinner and wine—and two desserts. That certainly seemed like interest to her.

Taking her cue from him, she took the other side of the couch, a little closer to the center than the end. She took a sip of the merlot. Fruity, easy on the tongue, with a long finish. Just how she liked it.

"So," he said. "About that baggage."

"Yours or mine?"

"Mine. I don't know yours." He smiled again, flashing the dimple in his cheek. "Plus, it's part of the apology."

"You're talking about your ex, right?" At the question on his face, she added, "Elinore told me a little bit about her."

"Was that before or after she told you not to break my heart?"

"She didn't get that far, but it was right after she told me she was a little protective of you. It was strongly implied."

"Big sisters," he said. "What can you do?"

"She said your ex was a piece of work."

He gave a bitter little bark of laughter. "Yeah, you might say that."

Listening to his story, she could tell he was trying for a just-the-facts delivery, but a jumble of emotions played across his face—a quagmire of confusion, pain, and bitterness Robbi knew all too well. As he talked, she felt it all with him. The initial jolt of attraction, followed by a whirlwind romance and a marriage that was crumbling well before it began. He just hadn't seen it. Except for the marriage part, it reminded her of her relationship with Jax. All the red flags had been there, but, like Mal, she'd chosen not to notice them.

He ducked his head when he told her about the two weeks he'd spent in jail, as if he were ashamed at having been arrested, even though the charges had been dropped. The faire had given him a haven, a place at first to hide and then to heal. As the story ended, he looked into her face like a man awaiting judgement. "When you said you wanted in on the wager, all I could think was, here we go again."

Robbi pulled herself out of that clear blue gaze and watched the wine swirl in her glass. "You don't even know what I was going to do if I won."

"What *were* you going to do if you won?"

"I don't know. I just wanted to buy some time. Everything was happening so fast."

He nodded, waiting for her to go on.

She set her glass down on the coffee table and turned toward him, tucking one leg under herself. "I still don't know. I mean, I don't want all of you to lose your homes, but I don't want to see Guy killed either. I think..." She paused, gathering her thoughts. "I've been wondering why Laura was buying those shares, and I think she was trying to keep Guy from being able to sell. So, I'm leaning that way too. You know, for her. And for all of you."

He set his glass down beside hers. "I don't want Guy to die either—even though I want to punch him sometimes. There has to be another way."

"What do we do about the wager, anyway? Wait until Guy heals? Tell him he rides or he loses, broken leg or not?" Her nose wrinkled. "That doesn't seem fair."

"When we brought him home yesterday, he seemed like he was taking himself out of the mix. If he still feels that way tomorrow, I guess his shares go into the pot and it's between you and me."

She shifted her weight sideways, so she was facing him.

What would she do if they went on with the competition and she won? If she pushed the sale of the faire, the money would give her a new start, but the Troupe would lose their little piece of paradise. The thought of Joanne packing up her forge and locking her cottage for the last time made Robbi feel a little queasy. It would be as bad or even worse for the others. Winner take all, Mal had said, which meant the McClarens, Cara, Dale, and Miller would walk away with nothing. For Dale, who had lost Laura too, it would be worse than nothing.

And if she kept things as they were? Assuming they could find a way to keep Guy alive, she'd probably be able to negotiate a portion of the gate sales. She could finish her thesis and then come back here to stay as long as she wanted to. The best of both worlds.

But if Mal won, she'd be the one to walk away with nothing.

He watched her wrestle with it, not speaking, just giving her time to think it through. She liked that he didn't rush her, liked that calm, solid presence that had given her comfort on her first terrible day here.

"If Guy withdraws, do we have to compete? Or can we come to an agreement?"

"I think that's up to us," he said. "What sort of agreement would we be coming to?"

MAL FELT a weight lift from his chest as they hammered it out together. First, they'd divide the shares so Robbi's vote would have the same weight as Mal's and Elinore's. Then they'd find a way to save Guy. If that meant selling, they'd pay Guy's debt and give the silent partner his due, then divide the rest evenly between Robbi and the Rennies. If they could find another way, things would go on as they were, with Guy at the helm but hobbled, unable to use the faire as gambling collateral. Robbi would get Laura's portion of the gate.

It was as fair a deal as they could make it, with the caveat that, when the killer was discovered, he—or she—got nothing.

"You do think they'll get caught, don't you?" Robbi said.

"I do. Sooner or later." He had to believe that. The thought of going on, day to day, knowing one of his friends might be a murderer was too unbearable to contemplate. He waited to see if she wanted to talk about it further. She leaned forward to pick up her wine glass, her wistful expression suggesting a distraction from murder and loss might be more welcome. He said, "About that baggage of yours..."

She took a sip of wine, then set her glass on the table. When she turned back to face him, she seemed to shift a half-inch closer. "What about it?"

"Your turn to share, if you want to."

Minus the jail time and the marriage, her story sounded familiar. She'd been gullible, just like he had, reliving old patterns, making excuses for the inexcusable. Those patterns, too, had common denominators. His father had been absent, hers adoring but unreliable, at least when it came to the marriage. Both their mothers were emotionally unstable, hers committing suicide when Robbi was a teenager, his succumbing to pneumonia in a mental institution when he was a child. Both he and Robbi had been introduced to literature as education and escape, she by her father, he by Elinore, whose thirst for books was second only to her thirst for making things and taking them apart.

That revelation led them to books, which led them to

movies, which led them to philosophy, their best and worst jobs, and their Ren Faire experiences. That led them back to Laura, but this time in a way that felt less of loss than of appreciation. They shared their favorite memories until Robbi's eyes were bright with laughter, and Mal thought if he didn't kiss her, he might regret it until the day he died.

He slid closer, resting his arm on the back of the couch. A junior high move, but there was nowhere else for it to go. He hesitated. Why had everything he'd brought had garlic in it?

She lifted her chin, and once again, he found himself caught up in the depths of her eyes.

Go on, Mal. Take a chance.

What were hearts for, if not for breaking?

Their lips were almost touching.

And then they did.

I USE my trademark weave between the legs to take the deputy down. He lands with a thud that knocks the breath out of him, and Tuck plows straight across him in his eagerness to get away. We cut through an alley, across two lawns, and down the next street before the man's curses fade into the distance and we finally feel safe.

The rush of adrenalin coincides with a rush of fondness for Tuck. I must say, the little chap came through when it counted. He's exuberant with victory. If this had been a football game—what most Americans call soccer—we would have won the World Cup and bought each other a round of excellent ale.

Soon enough, however, the euphoria fades. There are no convenient pickup trucks heading out of town. It's a long walk back to Robbi's cottage, and by the time we get there, the sun is a splinter of gold edging the tree line. Tuck's cheery demeanor has long since evaporated, and my patience is stretched as thin as air.

I bite my tongue to keep myself from telling him, "Tuck, you are no Watson."

CHAPTER FIFTEEN

It was almost sunrise when she heard Trouble come in through the window she'd left open for him. "Where have you been?" she murmured as he curled up at her feet and fell fast asleep.

He was still sleeping when she got up an hour later. She felt groggy from the wine and her late night with Mal, but there was a bubble of joy in her chest that she hadn't felt in a long time. By the time she'd flown and fed Falcor, then taken a long shower, she felt refreshed. She came out drying her hair and peeked in on Trouble. Still sleeping soundly. Whatever he'd been up to last night seemed to have worn him out.

She took a closer look. His fur, usually so shiny and sleek, was dull with dust and dotted with burrs. The pads of his paws looked tender. Whatever he'd done, it looked like he'd gone a long way to do it.

Her phone beeped to announce a text, then another.

The first was from Joanne: *How did it go last night?*

The second was from Mal: *Want to come over and see the lambs?*

One gorgeous blue-eyed Scotsman plus an unspecified number of fluffy, gangly, big-eyed baby sheep? What red-blooded woman would say no to that? She sent him a quick *yes,* then fretted over her response to Joanne. Everything she thought about seemed like too much or not enough. She settled on a thumbs up, followed by a heart, a hug and a *thanks*. It didn't begin to encompass what Joanne had done, considering her own feelings for Mal, but Robbi was pretty sure her friend would understand.

HER KNOCK WAS GREETED by Elinore's husky "Come in."

Robbi was pleased to see her awake and alert, if a bit wan, working on one of her contraptions at the kitchen table. "It's for Miller," Elinore said, "if he doesn't turn out to be a villain. He wanted a prototype for a machine to deliver sweets to children."

"Do you think he's a villain?" Robbi leaned in for a closer look at the device, which used a series of cogs, weights, and levers to deliver a pea-sized piece of bread dough from the end of a wooden tube.

"The final version will be bigger," Elinore said. "And instead of dough balls, he's going to use little marzipan creatures, like dragons and unicorns. That means there has to be enough force to get them to the end of the tube, but it has to be gentle enough not to squish them out of shape. It's quite the puzzle." She picked up the dough ball and looked at it with a critical eye. "But you asked about Miller. If I think he's a villain."

"Do you?"

The injured woman shrugged, wincing at the movement. "He could be, I suppose. He's an odd little bird, which makes him an easy person to suspect."

"But you don't think so?"

"I'm not like Mal," Elinore said. "Mal gets hurt and picks himself up, and after a while he forgets what that felt like and goes right back to trusting. He's the only person in this world I'd swear on my soul is not a villain." She ran a finger over a wooden cog. "Miller didn't ask me to make this machine because he trusts me, and I didn't say yes because I trust him. If he turns out to be the one who did this, I'll give his little prototype to whoever takes his place. In the meantime, I like the challenge."

They both looked up as Mal came through the back door and wiped his feet on the mat.

"Tuck's plum tuckered out," he said, shaping his brogue into a bad Southern twang. "He looks like he went on a five-mile hike last night."

"Trouble, too," Robbi said. "I wonder what they got themselves into."

"That cat," Elinore said, though her lips tugged upward in a smile. "He's a bad influence on our Tuck."

Mal snorted. "Tuck was a delinquent long before Trouble came along."

He came around the table and pulled Robbi to him for a kiss. It was little more than a peck, but it made Robbi's knees wobbly. He smelled like sandalwood and soap, with an underlayer of something delicious that was all him. She felt a rush of heat, along with the awareness that his bedroom was less than ten feet from where she was standing.

Reluctantly, he pulled away. "El, we're going out to see the lambs. Do you need anything before we go?"

"What? Not going to ask me if I want to come along?"

He grinned. "When you're engrossed in a project? What would be the point of that?"

Elinore waved them off with her good hand. "No point at all, so get on with your young selves, and let me get back to it."

Robbi had barely stepped off the stoop when he turned and drew her in for another kiss, a real one this time. She'd almost forgotten what a real kiss felt like, one that made you tingle in all the right places. From the hunger in his eyes, she thought maybe he'd almost forgotten too.

THEY STEPPED APART as Guy's car, a gun-metal gray Honda he'd traded his Lexus for, pulled to a stop in front. He'd cited practicality as the reason for the trade, but in retrospect, Mal supposed he should have suspected an ulterior motive. For all his generosity, Guy had never been much for deferred gratification.

Resisting the temptation to stake his claim by putting an arm around Robbi, Mal started toward the car. As far as he could tell, there was no reason for Guy to drive over when he could text. Surely, he couldn't finesse the pedals with his broken leg.

Then the driver's door opened, and Hammond stepped out. Guy clambered out the passenger side, pulling his crutches out behind him.

"What's going on?" Mal asked as Robbi came up beside him.

Guy glanced from one to the other, then settled himself

onto his crutches with an appraising tilt of the head. "Ham's driving me to meet with the developers. I'm going to see if I can get them to make an offer on the land we haven't built on yet."

"We had a deal," Mal pointed out, keeping his tone mild. "You might not even own that land. Or at least, you might not own the right to sell it."

Guy held up his hands. "I know, I know. I promise I won't sign anything."

"Although," Hammond pointed out, "if I recall, y'all didn't draw up any papers."

"It was a gentleman's agreement," Mal said, coolly. "Though I don't suppose you'd know much about that."

With a glower at Mal, Hammond started around the car.

"Hold on, hold on!" Guy snagged the sheriff's shirt as Hammond passed. "Mal's right. It was a gentleman's agreement. It's binding, morally at least, and probably legally. We have witnesses."

The sheriff rounded on Guy with a punch. Guy let go of his shirt and parried with one crutch, teetering on the other, as Mal moved between them.

He was quick, but Robbi was quicker, darting under his arm and coming up in the center of the three men like a dolphin surfacing for air. "That's enough," she said, then added sweetly, "Could we have a little less testosterone here, please?"

Guy hopped back, laughing and wincing at the same time. "Aye, m'lady."

Mal suppressed a smile. His fierce little falcon. He held his ground until, grudgingly, Hammond stepped back. Guy looked back at Mal and Robbi and said, "I'm just going to see what they'll offer. I came by because I wanted you to know."

Mal held up a hand. "What you said yesterday, about the wager?"

Guy sighed, looking so broken and defeated that Mal almost wished he hadn't brought it up. Almost.

Guy said, "I haven't changed my mind. If you break a leg during the Olympics, they don't put the games on hold until you're up to par."

Mal nodded, torn between relief at Guy's decision and regret that it had come to this. "You're a good man."

Guy tucked his crutches back under his arms, already turning toward the car. "I'm not. But I'm trying to be."

AS GUY'S Honda pulled away, Robbi laid a hand on Mal's back. His muscles were like knotted steel.

"Hey," she said. "Are you okay?"

"I'm fine."

He didn't sound angry, but he didn't sound fine, either. She said, "This is good, right? He's stepping aside. We can follow the plan."

He pulled his gaze away from the car as it disappeared around the Loop. "I don't like that Hammond is with him. Guy has good intentions, but that doesn't mean he can't be swayed."

"What is it with you two? Sometimes I think you're best friends, and sometimes I think you hate him."

He smiled, but it looked forced. "I'll let you know when I figure it out. Now, let's go play with some lambs."

WATCHING Robbi giggle at the antics of the two-week-old

lambs, Mal felt the tension drain from his shoulders. The babies clambered over her, nursing at her fingers, nibbling at her hair, nuzzling at her pockets for nuggets of oat cake.

"They should bottle this," she said. "We'd make a billion dollars selling cuteness in a jar."

"I like the way you think." He dropped onto the grass behind her, and she settled in against his back like she belonged there.

"Mal," she said, nuzzling a small muzzle with her cheek. "Why do you think Guy came here, instead of to Cara's? I mean, clearly she's crazy about him."

"A little too crazy, maybe. I like Cara, but Guy's a free spirit, and she's made it clear she's ready to snap on a leash."

"Did you know she used to work as a magician's assistant? The Great Fallini."

"Never heard of him."

"They had a knife-throwing act. She 'accidentally' killed him during practice." She extracted a finger from a lamb's mouth and made air quotes with her fingers.

He bent his head to rest his chin against her hair. It was still damp and smelling of some flowery shampoo. For a moment, he let himself get lost in it. Then he pulled his mind back to the conversation at hand. He didn't want to think of any of the Rennies killing anyone. Not Cara, not Dale, not even Miller, whom he'd always thought of as innocuous and a little annoying. If there was a killer—and in light of Guy's *accidents* and the attack on Elinore, there clearly must be—Mal wanted it to be some malevolent stranger. Or maybe an evil spirit from an ancient burial ground.

Or Hammond.

The phone in his pocket buzzed. Ignore it, he told himself.

Instead, he pulled it out and looked at the caller ID. "It's Guy," he said.

"Already?" She sat up straight and scooted around to look. The lambs swarmed around her, and she handed out a handful of oat nuggets to appease them.

He tapped the *answer* button, and Guy's voice came on the line, his words pouring out in such a panicked rush that Mal could only catch half of them: "Car crashed...no brakes...I think...sheriff's dead."

CHAPTER SIXTEEN

I'm awakened by a pounding at the door. I tuck my head under Robbi's pillow and wait for the pounding to stop. When it doesn't, it becomes clear that Robbi has gone someplace without me. I don't know whether to be grateful for the extra bit of a kip, or annoyed at having been left behind. I decide on the former when I realize she's left a bit of grilled halibut in my bowl. I bolt it down and, still a bit disgruntled at my interrupted sleep, hop out the open window to see what's up.

For the second time since Robbi's arrival, deputies are gathering the Troupe into the King's Moot. When I arrive, Robbi and Mal are already seated at one of the long tables. On Mal's other side, Elinore sits stiffly, her hands in her lap. Still sore, no doubt, from the arrow wound.

Guy sits across from them, his broken leg stuck out at the end of the bench, his crutches propped against the table. Our dashing young swashbuckler looks worse for wear, with a new bruise on one cheek and a cut on his forehead. One of his eyes is beginning to blacken.

Despite their obvious concern, there's a new energy between Robbi and Mal. For the first time since Mal proposed his wager, they seem to be enjoying each other's company. No need to wonder what they've got up to since I left on my little adventure with Tuck.

Speaking of Tuck, I glance around to see if he's up and about. Sure enough, he's under the table between Elinore and Mal. He looks every bit as knackered as I feel, and I'm glad I didn't vent my frustration on him on our journey back from town.

Dale and Joanne enter with one deputy, followed a few minutes later by Miller and Cara. She squeezes in between Dale and Guy, while Miller takes a seat away from the rest of the group. No one looks happy.

When the gang's all here, Acting Sheriff Debba Holt assigns a burly man with a crew cut to keep order among the group while she interviews them one at a time in Guy's office. From her announcement to the Troupe, I glean that there's been an accident. While Debba explains the failure of Guy's brakes, Guy traces the wood grain of the table with a finger.

He looks the picture of misery, perhaps because of the damage to himself and his car, perhaps because Sheriff Hammond, who was driving, is in critical condition.

Foul play is suspected.

Not an accident at all, then. Does this mean Hammond is not the killer? I can't imagine he would have gotten into a vehicle he himself had sabotaged.

While Debba decides who to interview first, I stroll into her office, find a shaft of sunlight to bask in, and settle down to groom myself. I look like a vagrant, and it will take some time to restore my coat to its usual elegance.

IT WAS STARTING to feel like Groundhog Day. Not in the madcap, entertaining way of the Bill Murray movie, but in the slogging through molasses way of a bad dream you can't wake up from. Poor Guy looked like he'd been mugged by a kangaroo.

"What's happened now?" Dale asked, with a sidelong glance toward Deputy Crew Cut, who was slowly scrolling down the screen of his mobile phone. "It looks like everybody's here, at least."

Robbi heard his unspoken conclusion: at least no more of them had been murdered.

"Guy's hurt," Cara said, stroking the arm of the man she seemed to have decided was the love of her life, whether he wanted to be or not. "This is getting out of hand."

"What are you talking about?" Dale snapped. "It got out of hand the minute Laura died." He clamped his mouth shut as if afraid of what else he might say.

Robbi glanced at Mal. She was pretty sure he'd back her play, but she wasn't sure she was right to play it. If she was wrong, she was revealing a secret that wasn't hers. But if she was right, didn't they all have a right to know? She turned back to Cara. "Guy's been awfully lucky lately, for a man someone keeps trying to kill."

Cara's eyes went flat, but Guy gave a stifled laugh and gestured to his cast. "Right now, I'm not feeling very lucky."

In a brittle voice, Cara said, "Are you implying something?"

"The Great Fallini," Robbi said. "Didn't he have a series of unfortunate accidents just before the one that killed him?"

"Great Fallini?" Guy looked from Robbi to Cara. "Who's he?"

Ignoring Guy's question, Cara jabbed a finger in the air. "One accident. And I didn't even pour that juice. You want to know what happened to the Great Fallini?"

"Yes, please." Robbi was glad to know her voice sounded stronger than she felt. "His daughter said you were—"

"I know what she said. She was wrong then, and she's wrong now." A pair of pink blotches bloomed on her cheeks. "And you're wrong too. I would never hurt Guy."

Quietly, Guy said, "It's all right, Cara. Just tell us what happened."

"He was a bully, that's what happened," she said, in a voice choked with indignation. "He taught me how to do the act, and the better I got at it, the more he hated it. I'd have left, but I needed the job. The day he—" She took a hitching breath and wiped her eyes. Shot a glance toward the deputy, who seemed to be paying them no mind. She lowered her voice anyway. "The day he died, he'd been berating me all morning. Vicious things. Said I was worthless. That teaching me was the biggest mistake of his life. When I was on the wheel, he nicked me three times with the knives, and every time, he said it was my fault. He said I'd moved."

"Throwing knives," Robbi clarified for the group. "The Wheel of Death."

Cara nodded. "By the time it was my turn to throw, I was a wreck. I was shaking so hard I could hardly hold the knives. I told him I couldn't do it, that I was bound to miss. He said I'd better throw, and throw well, or I was fired." Her expression hardened. "So I threw."

Guy folded his hand over hers. Considering it hadn't been established she wasn't the one who was trying to kill him, Robbi found it a remarkably sweet gesture. "It wasn't your fault," he said. "You tried to warn him."

Elinore gave Cara an appraising look. "If she's telling the truth."

. . .

Acting Sheriff Debba has no better luck than her predecessor at ferreting out the culprit. Miller is no less timid, Dale no less affable, Elinore no less prickly, and Joanne no less adversarial. Cara seems more flustered than before, which I attribute to her concern for Guy and her emotions regarding the Great Fallini. Robbi, of course, is more composed than she was for her first interview, but then, that day, she'd just had an awful shock.

By the time Mal comes in, I've nearly returned my coat to its usual splendor.

"So," Debba says, "I'm told you're good with cars."

Mal shrugs. "I'm good at lots of things."

"Don't mess with me," she says. "I hear you have a grudge against Guy."

Mal's having none of that. "He risked our futures on a hand of poker. Don't tell me I'm the only one with a grudge against Guy."

She leans back in Guy's chair and clasps her hands behind her head. "I heard he defiled your sister, once upon a time."

Mal laughs. "Defiled? Elinore's a big girl. Who she has a romp with is no concern of mine."

"Maybe not," Debba says, leaning forward as if to give the words more gravitas, "but since attempts were made on both their lives, it seems to concern someone."

"Let's face it," Joanne said. She brushed an invisible crumb from her blacksmith's apron. "It could be any of us."

"No, it couldn't," Dale said.

"But it could. We all have things that make us seem suspicious. I've got a temper, Cara's—obviously—got a past. Even you, Dale. The boyfriend is always a suspect. We all had motive. We all had opportunity. Like today's accident. Guy, you said your brakes failed?" At his nod, she went on. "When was the last time you drove your car?"

"I don't know. Last week sometime."

"Right. So it could have been sabotaged any time between then and now. Any of us could have done it." She pointed at Cara. "You, me, even Miller."

"Miller?" Mal laughed. "He wouldn't know a brake line from an oil pan."

Elinore rolled her eyes. "He isn't stupid. He could have learned it on YouTube. Any of us could."

Dale splayed his hands flat on the table. Musician's hands, long and slim, callused at the fingertips. "We could have, but we didn't. Only one of us did. *Maybe* one of us did. But now we look at each other, and we're all thinking, 'Is it you? Or maybe you?' Even if—or when—we catch this guy, how can we go back to how things were? I'm always going to know some of you wonder if I killed the only woman I ever loved, and you're always going to know I'm wondering the same thing about you."

"Trust is a fragile thing," Joanne said. "It's easy to break, hard to repair. A thing like this, it shows us where the fractures are. If what we have here is worth saving, we have to use that knowledge to make it better than it was. Repair the fractures. Deeper friendships, stronger ties."

"I don't know if I can." Dale looked down at his hands and added quietly. "I don't know if any of us can."

Robbi looked over at Miller. He sat at a table as far from the group as he could get. Shoulders slumped, he stared down at his steepled fingers, ignoring—or pretending to ignore—the conversation at the other table. What must his life have been like, Robbi wondered, if this was the closest thing he had to a home? A misfit among misfits. If he was the guilty party, he deserved it, but if he wasn't...

"Miller?" Robbi called. When he looked up, she patted the bench beside her. "Why don't you come over here and join us?"

He looked up, hope and suspicion warring on his face. Then he slowly came over and plopped down at the table, looking like he'd just been invited to hang out with the cool kids.

WHEN THE INTERVIEWS are finally finished, I make my way over to Tuck. It doesn't take a famous detective to see he's had enough investigating for one day. Poor bloke. It's not his fault he hasn't got the stamina for real detective work; my paws are as sore as his hooves, but when duty calls, I serve at Her Majesty's pleasure.

I spend the rest of the afternoon eavesdropping on the suspects and searching for Laura's journal and a murder weapon. The challenge is not so much in finding plausible weapons, but rather in eliminating all the rest. So many things can cause a head wound, from marble bookends to common rocks. Not to mention the plethora of axes, swords, and cudgels lying about.

In the wake of the bookshelf incident, Cara is vigilant against intrusion. I shall have to be more resourceful if I mean to get inside again. At the McClaren cottage, Elinore tries to distract me from my mission with a bit of string, as if I were a common cat.

I stop by Miller's for a spot of tea. He gives me cream and kidneys, and while I eat, I notice a wrinkled, tear-stained paper on a shelf behind the counter. This must be the one he was reading the first time I came here, the one he'd so hurriedly shoved into his pocket.

I pull it toward me and realize it's a poem. A love poem, to be exact.

"I see you, my love,

In my heart, in my dreams,

But you do not see me."

He wads it up and tosses it into the bin before I can read the rest, but I've seen enough. This confirms his unrequited feelings for Laura.

When Miller sends me on my way with a final bite of kidney, I visit Joanne at the barn, where she's patching a matching pair of nicks, one in the feed room door, the other in its frame. She bends to give me a scratch on the chin and sighs. "It must have happened when we were getting the lances ready for the joust. I wish people would be more careful."

I leave her to her work and continue my search.

I am thorough. I am vigilant. But no matter where I go, I see no sign of Laura's journal.

CHAPTER SEVENTEEN

The sky was awash with purple and gold when Robbi made it to the meadow the next morning, her kestrel on her hand. She launched the bird twice, using the leather bat lure to draw him back in. Then she gave him the signal for free hunting and walked the edge of the meadow, kicking at bushes to flush out the insects and small rodents. Falcor circled, then plunged. He snapped up a grasshopper, then lit on a nearby branch to enjoy his well-earned snack.

When Robbi looked up again, Guy was standing at the edge of the field. When he realized she'd seen him, he picked his way carefully toward her, his crutches making little pockmarks in the earth.

"What happened with Cara?" she asked. "I can't decide if telling you all about the Great Fallini was a good idea."

"Hard to say." He gave her a winsome smile. "My take is, better to get it over with than keep it in and let it fester 'til it grows all out of proportion. Like ripping off a Band-Aid, to use a metaphor."

"That's not a metaphor. That's a simile."

"Whatever." He dismissed the error with a wave, then looked down, shuffling his feet like a schoolboy. "Look, there's something I've been wanting to tell you."

"Oh?"

"I–"

Miss Scarlett's cheerful bark cut through the trees, heralding the arrival of Mal and his four-legged entourage. Robbi couldn't stop a grin from spreading across her face, while Guy flashed a smile that couldn't quite hide his disappointment at the moment lost.

Robbi sent Falcor on one final loop, then called him back to her hand. This was what she loved about falconry, that the kestrel could at any time be free by simply not returning when she called.

Mal nodded toward Guy, not quite friendly, not quite not. "That's some shiner you're working on there."

Gingerly, Guy touched a finger to his eye, as if he'd forgotten about the bruises. "I've been thinking. You were right yesterday. I have been lucky. But I don't think I can be lucky forever."

"No," Robbi said. "No one can."

"They aren't going to stop, whoever they are. I found this dropped inside my mail slot this morning." He pulled a folded paper from his pocket and held it out.

Mal took it and read aloud, "'If you want this to be over, meet me at midnight inside the old mill.'" He handed it back to Guy. "You aren't thinking of going?"

Guy folded the paper and put it back in his pocket. "It's either that or wait for them to try again. Sooner or later, they're going to succeed."

"Maybe not," Robbi said. "The poisoning was a near thing, but if they'd used more, you might not have made it long enough for Trouble and Tuck to find you. There was no guarantee you'd be hurt badly, or at all, in the fall from your horse, and you could have either died in that car wreck or walked away without a scratch. Maybe they don't want to succeed. Maybe they just want you to need them."

"You mean Cara?" Guy said. "I can't say you're wrong, but it seems risky. I mean, if I die, that pretty much tanks any chance of a relationship."

"Maybe she doesn't care. Maybe, given the choice, she'd rather make you need her, but she'd rather lose you completely than see you with someone else."

He cocked his head as if evaluating her words. "You didn't believe her explanation about Fallini?"

"I don't know if I believe it. It sounded plausible, but even if it's true, one doesn't preclude the other. She could still be setting up all these accidents to make herself indispensable to you."

"Or it could be somebody different altogether." He held out his hands like a scale and made a weighing motion. "The good thing is, if it's her and I meet her at the mill, I can probably handle her."

"Unless she shoots you."

"I have to do something," Guy said. "It's starting to feel like I really have something to be afraid of."

"Being poisoned should probably have told you that." Robbi reached for the note. *If you want this to be over.* It sounded ominous. "Have you showed this to Deputy—I mean, Acting Sheriff Debba?"

"She was Ham's right-hand man. Person. I don't trust her."

Which was probably wise, given what they knew of Hammond.

“Well, you can’t go to this meeting,” Mal said. “That leg puts you at a huge disadvantage.”

They all considered the options. After a while, Mal said, “Look, what if you could go and not go at the same time?”

Guy laughed. “What, you have a Tardis somewhere? Or a time machine?”

“More like a clone. I put on a cloak and a fake cast, and I go as you. I’ll get a confession on my cell phone if I can, and if I have to fight, they’ll be expecting you to be crippled by that leg. I can take them by surprise.”

“Wait a minute,” Robbi said. “I don’t like this plan at all.”

There were a million ways it could go wrong, and all of them ended up with Mal wounded or dead. She liked Guy, but sacrificing Mal for him was something she wasn’t prepared to do.

“It will be fine,” Mal said, with a reassuring smile. “It’s time for us to get proactive.”

MAL WOKE up fifteen minutes before the alarm. Quarter to eleven. Truth to tell, he hadn’t slept much at all, thinking of all the things that could go wrong, planning for contingencies. What if there was more than one assailant? What if they brought guns? What if they were wearing vests full of dynamite? It wasn’t likely, but it was possible. Almost anything was. He tried to make a rough plan for each contingency, knowing that whatever happened, it would likely be something he’d never imagined.

He thought of the old saw: No plan survives first contact with the enemy. He knew it was true.

The house was dark, silent save for the ticking of the clock and Miss Scarlett's breathing. Elinore had taken a pain pill and should sleep soundly until morning, but he wrote her a note anyway and left it on the kitchen table, just in case the worst thing happened and he didn't make it home.

He changed into dark clothes and a maroon cloak Guy had given him. Then he wrapped his right leg in cotton batting until it looked as thick as Guy's cast. He practiced limping until he thought he had it right, but then he realized he'd need Guy's crutches and grabbed a walking stick for Guy to use in their stead. The last thing he did before leaving the house was check the charge on his phone. One hundred percent. Good to go.

He slipped out of the house with Scarlett at his heels. Tuck met him at the front stoop.

He followed the Loop until he reached the access road to the mill. Then he skirted the *Danger! Condemned! Do Not Enter!* sign and picked his way through the woods with his cell phone's flashlight. He was early, but Robbi and Guy were earlier. Trouble perched on a fallen log where he could get a good view.

Robbi came into his arms and gave him a long squeeze. "Please don't get yourself killed."

"I won't." He tipped up her chin and kissed her, long and deep, the kind of kiss a man might go to war for. "Promise me, if things go wrong, you won't put yourself in harm's way."

She pulled away. "You mean don't do what you're doing? Mal, I'm not promising you that."

Guy said, "I'll keep her safe. You have my word. It's the least I can do."

"You guys," Robbi said. "Let's just all agree to look out for each other."

Mal nodded. "You know what to do. You'll keep Scarlett and Tuck here. If someone runs out of the mill, take them down and restrain them until we can get the sheriff out here. If someone comes up, let them go in. Then wait for them to come out and implement plan A."

He studied the mill. It looked dark and brooding, canted to one side as if a strong wind might turn it into kindling. Behind it, he could see the river, black and rushing, churning with whitecaps. It looked like the Midgard serpent.

He pulled up his hood and tucked a crutch under each arm. Then he gave Robbi another reassuring smile. "Here we go."

Tuck and Miss Scarlett would be dead giveaways that Mal is an imposter, but on a darkish night, a sleek black cat can slink inside an unlit building without being seen. Mal doesn't notice me creeping along behind him, or if he does, he doesn't acknowledge me. He hesitates outside the door, then pushes it open and steps inside.

The millhouse has the feel of a long-empty building. No breath moves the air; there is no sense of living energy. The room is dark, but shafts of moonlight stream through chinks in the walls, revealing hulking shapes and shadows. My eyes are sharp, adjusting more quickly to the dark than my human companion. Ropes, pulled taut, run around and through the rafters and pillars. Blades of all kinds seem suspended from the walls, part of some intricate network of cogs and ropes and levers. The whole place is held together by nothing but a web of pressure and tension.

One fact shines bright and clear: This is a trap.

I give a warning yowl just as Mal steps toward the center of the room. I hear the click of a pressure plate beneath his boot. Then a heavy panel slams down, blocking the door. Gears begin to grind. A shadow swoops toward him, a glint of sharp steel in the moonlight, and he drops flat on his stomach as the blade of a battle axe grazes his hood.

"Oh, no," he groans. "Elinore."

ROBBI CHECKED HER WATCH AGAIN. Eleven fifty-eight. Maybe whoever had sent the message had somehow figured out their ploy and decided not to come. Or maybe they were already inside, and Mal was busy teasing out a confession. She couldn't hear voices over the tumbling river.

Then running footsteps sounded on the path, and a figure dressed in white burst into the clearing, a mane of wild hair flowing behind her.

Elinore?

The woman raced past their hiding place without a sideways glance, fully focused on the millhouse. "Mal!" Her voice rose higher, panicked. "Mal, stop!"

Robbi flashed an open palm toward Scarlett—"Stay!"—and bolted from the trees in time to snag the back of Elinore's nightgown. Scarlett shot past her, racing toward the mill, but there was nothing Robbi could do about that. She couldn't stop them both. She could hear Guy picking his way through the undergrowth with Mal's walking stick.

Elinore tried to jerk free, and when that failed, flung a wild blow at Robbi's head. "Let me go. I've got to—"

"Hold on, hold on. It's all right, he's all right." Wrangling the distraught woman was like trying to wrestle an eel.

"It's not all right, you stupid little tart!" Elinore shrieked. "I've got to get him out of there!"

Robbi held on tight. "Elinore, stop. He knows what he's doing."

Elinore spun around and clapped a hand to each of Robbi's cheeks. "What don't you understand? The mill is booby trapped!"

Robbi blinked. "What? How do you know?"

"We don't have time for this," Elinore said. She spun on Guy as he finally hobbled onto the trail behind them. "This is all your fault!"

THE TRAP IS SPRUNG. The axe blade thunks through a central rope. Both ends snap back, and the web of ropes and cables begins to unravel. Every hair on my body raises as the air fills with the creak and snap of breaking wood. All four walls shift and sway. I hear the monstrous shriek of heavy beams under impossible stress, then a roar like thunder as one beam, then another, topples in a rain of rubble.

A shard of moonlight widens, a gap opening in the wall beside me. I leap through it to safety as a blur of red—Miss Scarlett!—hurtles past me in the opposite direction. Faithful, foolish dog.

Glancing back, I catch a glimpse of her plume-like tail. Then the millhouse collapses like a house of oversized pickup sticks.

CHAPTER EIGHTEEN

Elinore let out a banshee wail as Robbi stared aghast at what was left of the old mill. Her body felt frozen, but her mind was racing. If this was a movie, Mal would have seen it coming and dived out of a window or taken shelter under a conveniently arranged pile of old grindstones. But this wasn't a movie, and no one was guaranteed a happy ending.

She couldn't just give up, though. She'd watched enough movies to know that no one was dead until you actually saw the body. With a little sob of laughter, she recalled how she and Laura used to call that old trope Schrodinger's corpse.

She shoved Elinore out of her way and pelted toward the mill, tears mixing with the haze of dust and sawdust falling on her face.

Then she was clawing at the rubble, flinging away shards of wood and shingle, barely noticing the splinters in her palms.

Mal, you stupid, gallant idiot, you promised me you wouldn't die.

A hand fell on her shoulder. Elinore, her panic replaced by

a deathly calm, said, "There's still a chance. He could still be all right."

"What?" Robbi wiped sweat and sawdust from her eyes. "How could anyone survive that?"

"Because." Elinore looked at the ruined building with a hint of a smile. "It was a very elaborate trap."

I FIND Tuck grieving near the tree line, and teeter on the edge of decision. Send the pig for help or go myself? I'm faster, but I'm also lighter and more nimble. My skills may be of better use here.

I reassure him there may still be hope—after all, earthquake survivors have been found days after having been buried in a building collapse. Surely Mal stands a chance under a pile of rotting wood.

And swords and circular saws and axes, my mind reminds me, but I don't share this with Tuck. Instead, I tell him to bring Joanne, Freyja, Falcor, and a stout rope. Fast.

He doesn't think Falcor will come, but I suggest he tell the kestrel Robbi needs him. He may or may not be of use. Birds of prey are still essentially barbarians.

I hurry back to what's left of the old mill and leap onto the fallen beams, listening for sounds of life and searching for a way in. I'm finally at the river's edge beside the ruined water wheel when I hear the unmistakable whimper of a dog.

HIS MIND SWAM out of darkness into a world that was wet and freezing. Something kept tugging at him, something dangerous; but someone he loved was there beside him, a comforting presence. It whimpered near his ear. Slowly, a name came to him. Scarlett.

Awareness came back gradually. He was in some kind of cage, submerged, or mostly submerged, in water cold enough to make his teeth chatter and rough enough to pitch the cage from side to side. It was like being rocked to sleep by a giant toddler in a state of mania. He tried to touch bottom, but he couldn't feel his legs. His arms were useless too, floating beside him like a pair of pool noodles.

God, no.

A wave washed across his face. He coughed and sputtered, and was lifted. Scarlett, he thought again, and realized that the only thing keeping his head above water was his dog. She paddled steadily beside him, the front of his shirt clenched in her teeth. Her eyes were determined but exhausted, and he could tell the current and his extra weight were slowly wearing her down.

What the hell had happened?

While Guy and Elinore help Robbi try to clear a path to Mal, I find a small hole that gives me a glimpse of him. He's conscious, but barely. There's an ugly gash on his forehead. I realize he's in some kind of cage. There must have been a trap door of some sort that kept him from being caught in the collapse.

I can't help but feel a smidge of admiration for Elinore. Only a true Moriarty could have dreamed up such a scheme.

The cavalry begins to arrive, first Joanne with Freyja and the rope, then Falcor, who takes up a position in the trees. Tuck scurries off again, returning with Cara in a man's long shirt and leggings, Dale in jeans and a pajama shirt, and even little Miller, his bald head shining in the moonlight.

Robbi gives one end of the rope to Joanne and takes the other for herself. She puts a hand on the rubble, but when she starts to climb, the beams beneath her shift and teeter. The mass is too unstable, even for a human of her size. She tries another place and then another, now sobbing in frustration.

I pick my way back to her and look into her face, voicing a tiny meow.

I can do it, my meow says. Let me help you save him.

Humans are difficult to communicate with. Typically, they're not good listeners, and they never understand how to speak cat, but she did trust me to help her cook the fish, and even though she doesn't know if Mal is alive or dead, or how even a clever cat might be of help, I'm hoping she'll trust me now.

She bends close and kisses the top of my head. "Bring him back to me," she says, and offers the rope.

I take it in my mouth, and before you can say Bob's your uncle, I'm back in position, snaking the rope down through the hole toward Mal.

FEELING RETURNED TO HIS FINGERS, first a tingle, then the sting of a thousand needles. He welcomed the pain. He welcomed it all, as his body slowly came back to life.

When he'd regained enough mobility, he explored the cage and found no way out. The latch and lock were high-quality and tamper-proof, and the seams where the sides met were firmly attached. In time, if he didn't die of exposure first, he was sure he'd find a solution. For now, it was his turn to support Scarlett, holding onto the cage with one hand and cradling her in the other arm. His lower back felt like someone had smashed him from behind with a sledgehammer, but he needed to help her save her strength. Who knew how long they'd have to tread water before someone figured out how to rescue them?

Robbi's plaintive voice came back to him: *Promise me you won't get yourself killed.* He had to get back to her.

A stern meow came from overhead, and a moment later, the end of a rope dropped onto the cage.

Trouble?

Mal fumbled with the rope one-handed, looping it through the bars where the top met the corner of the cage and knotting it. It took three tries—he seemed to have lost much of his dexterity—but at last he had it. He gave it a tug to test its strength. It felt fine. Then he gave the rope another tug to tell whoever was on the other end that he was ready.

ROBBI HALF-SOBBED, half-laughed. That tug on the rope was like a message from Heaven. It meant Mal was alive. Not only alive, but conscious. It meant he might come back to her whole.

Joanne tied the rope to Freyja's harness, and now she asked the big mare to back up. The rope went taut. Then the rubble around Mal's end of the rope began to shift. Something emerged from the debris, a rectangular box with bars and mesh on the sides. Was that Mal inside? And was that Scarlett? Why did it have to be so dark?

Slowly, the cage rose out of the rubble. Then Freyja jerked to a halt.

"Back," Joanne said, pressing two fingers to the horse's chest. The mare strained to step backward, but the cage didn't move. "It's stuck on something."

Robbi picked a spot in front of Freyja and grabbed the rope

with both hands. She couldn't add much weight, but she was strong. "We've almost got it," she called to the Troupe. "Come on!"

They all piled on, in a deadly serious tug-of-war. Even Guy was pulling, standing on one leg, using the other for balance. The muscles in Robbi's arms begin to tremble. Then, with a sharp crack, the rubble shifted. Her spirits rose, then fell, as the cage slid out of its hole and caught again. It hung, half-suspended, between the rope and whatever had caught it by one edge.

"One more time!" Dale yelled. "Pull!"

With a shriek of metal, the cage separated into two pieces, one wall held firmly by the remains of the ruined mill. The rest of the cage jerked free. It bounced hard against the jumble of debris with a force that sent Scarlett tumbling from the open side. With a little yelp, she splashed into the water below.

Mal, of course, dived in after.

The Troupe breaks into pandemonium. Joanne rushes to unknot the rope. The others stumble along the shoreline, calling out to Mal in panicked voices.

Tuck follows, his sad little oinks almost lost in the din.

Only I see the small bald man, so consumed by terror he can barely walk, totter to the bank and, every muscle in his body quivering, leap in.

Mal was in the belly of the serpent. The current tugged and tumbled him, battering his bruised body until he'd lost all sense of where he was. One shoulder smashed against a rock. A jolt of pain shot through him, and the current drove him down and sent him spinning.

He came up coughing, then found his breath and finally his rhythm. It was a little like body surfing, which he'd done a few times in Europe as a boy, though never with his body so close to exhaustion. He caught a flash of Scarlett's white muzzle and swam for that until his fingers closed around her ruff and her collar. Then he adjusted his trajectory and aimed for shore, swimming one-armed and at a diagonal, not fighting the current, but slowly making his way across it.

He grabbed for a sapling and missed. The next, he caught for half a second before it slipped from his grasp. Not far ahead, he spied a fallen tree, its moonlit branches spreading out into the water. This time, he grabbed and held.

It took all his strength to push Scarlett up onto the bank. Then he dug deep and summoned a little more, pouring the effort into the fist clenched tight around a branch. Time disappeared. There was only water and darkness, the clenched fist, and his promise to Robbi.

As if from far away, he heard Robbi's voice, and Elinore's. Then a host of familiar hands pried his fingers from the branch and pulled him from the water.

I RACE ALONG THE SHORELINE, watching Miller bounce and flail, his voice no more than a petrified squeak above the roar of the river. No one knows he's there.

Around a bend, I see the others pulling Mal onto dry land. Miss Scarlett is already on shore. Her head droops, but her tail is wagging, albeit in slow motion. I launch myself into the middle of the group and bat at the rope looped around Joanne's shoulder.

"Hey, stop that!" she yells, but Robbi asks, "What? Trouble, what is it?"

I yowl to tell her Miller is in need of rescue, but she doesn't understand.

I hear a whoosh of air behind me. Then a blur of feathers swoops past Joanne's shoulder. Falcor snatches up the free end of the rope, then sails up and over the river, where he drops it squarely into Miller's grasping hand.

CHAPTER NINETEEN

"Miller, you idiot!" Joanne hauled the little man out of the water by his shirt and dumped him on the bank. "How did you end up in the river?"

Miller flushed, twisting his hands together as if he were working dough. "I kn...kn...know how you feel about him. I thought if I s...saved him..." He lowered his head onto his knees and mumbled, "I l...l...love you."

Robbi's mouth dropped open.

Joanne roared, "You what?"

"I said I...love you, Joanne." Now that the dam was open, the flood of words poured out. "I've always loved you. I was n...never looking at Laura. I was looking at you. You're...you're m...m....m...magnificent!"

"Miller...." Joanne shook her head as if in disbelief. "Are you saying you jumped in the river on purpose? To save Mal? For me?"

Before Miller could answer, Dale raised his hand as if he

were in grade school. "Um. This is nice and all, but...what the heck just happened? What was all that stuff with the mill?"

"That," said Elinore, "was justice. And it was brilliant." She punched Mal gently on the arm. "It was my *piece de resistance*, until you ruined it. I almost lost you!"

"El," he said, in a voice full of hurt, "you almost killed me."

"I know. But it wasn't meant for you. You shouldn't have even been there." She shot Robbi a sour look. "Did *she* put you up to it?"

Mal laid a protective hand on Robbi's arm. "I put myself up to it. Guy may have made mistakes, but he doesn't deserve to die."

"So you say." She looked at Guy. "Are you going to tell them? Because if you aren't, I will."

"Tell us what?" Robbi asked. "Guy, what's going on?"

"It was an accident," he said. He scanned the group with pleading eyes, then turned to Robbi. "I didn't even know she was there."

She. It took a moment for that to sink in. Was he talking about Laura? A chill spread through her body. Oh, ye gods and goddesses, he was.

He couldn't meet her gaze. "I've been trying to tell you for weeks. We kept getting interrupted."

"But you didn't." Would it have mattered if he had? He'd taken her best friend from her, a wrong that could never be righted. In a dull voice, she said, "How did it happen?"

His shoulders slumped. "You know I liked to practice at the old mill. I was working on a spinning sword strike. I had my earbuds in and didn't even hear her come up behind me. I did the move and there she was. My sword caught her in the head, and she went down in a heap. I tried to do CPR, but..." His voice broke. "She was already gone."

Guy.

Guy had killed Laura. She felt Mal press against her back, a comforting presence. "Why didn't you call 911?"

"I panicked and called Ham. Sheriff Hammond. He said it was too late to help her, and to put her in the river. If there was evidence, the water would wash it, or most of it, away, and he'd convince the coroner to say it was an accident. Which it was, just not the kind he wanted it to look like."

"Why? Why would he do that?"

"The developers," Mal said in a voice thick with disgust. "He didn't want his business partner going to jail before the deal went through."

Softly, Dale asked, "Why was she coming to see you, wearing that dress?"

Guy gave a little bark of laughter. "It's not what you think. It was going to be her wedding dress. She couldn't show you. That would be bad luck. But she was too excited not to tell someone, so she was going to show me and then Mal." Anticipating the next obvious question, he added, "She wrote about it in her diary before she left the house."

"Her diary?" Robbi said. "She had it with her? What did you do with it?"

"I got it from her cottage, in case she'd mentioned who she was going to see. I hid it in the castle, in one of the artifacts." Again, he scanned the group, as if looking for allies. Robbi didn't think he was going to find any. "You believe me, right?" he said. "You have to know I'd never hurt Laura on purpose."

"El?" Mal said. "You knew all this?"

"I saw it happen." Elinore crossed her arms and glared at Guy. "Tuck had escaped again, and I was looking for him everywhere. I wound up at the mill just as Guy decked Laura with his sword."

Robbi pushed the image away from her mind. "Why didn't you call the police?"

With a bitter laugh, Elinore said, "What would be the point of that? We'd just get Hammond, and we all know how that one goes."

"You could have told us," Mal said. "You could have told me."

"And have you do what? I love you, little brother, but you don't have the grit to do what needed to be done. Neither do your friends."

Trouble rubbed against Robbi's leg. She picked him up and buried her face in his fur. He smelled sweet, like comfort. "Was it like he said? An accident?"

Elinore shrugged. "It looked like that to me. But then he made a phone call, and right after that, he dumped her in the river. It was wrong. He should have been honest about it. Like he should have been honest about the shares. Like he should have been honest about—" She stopped, her cheeks flushing pink.

"I was always honest about that," Guy said softly. "I've lied about a lot of things, but never that."

Elinore shot him a blistering glare. "You had so many chances. You could have confessed after you survived the poison. You could have confessed after your stirrup broke, or after the car wreck. You could have faced up to what you did. That was the message. Come clean or die."

"But..." Robbi frowned, trying to make sense of it. "Any of those things could have killed him. It wasn't like you gave him the chance to make it right first, and then tried to kill him if he made the wrong choice."

"Don't you get it?" Elinore said. Robbi wondered if Mal had seen that same mad gleam in their mother's eyes, that same eagerness to explain the unexplainable. "That's the beauty of it. The element of chance. Chance put Laura in Guy's path at exactly the wrong time, so let chance determine Guy's fate. If the poison kills him, justice is served. If it doesn't, mercy wins. He has another opportunity to do the right thing."

"And if he doesn't, Chance gets another shot at him?"

"Exactly." Elinore smiled. "It's like letting the gods decide."

"ALL RIGHT," Mal says. "I get that Guy was responsible for Laura's death, and you were the one who tried to kill Guy, but who tried to kill you?"

I know the answer even before Joanne says, "She did it herself, to keep from being a suspect. But I have no idea how she did it. Pretty hard to stab yourself in the back."

Elinore smiles, an enigmatic Mona Lisa smile, and says, "A woman has to keep some secrets."

But it's not much of a secret to a world-famous detective. It's taken me longer than I would have liked, but I finally parse it out. The scratches in the arrow nock and the nicks in Joanne's feed room door frame tell the tale. She used the door to hold the arrow in place while she backed up onto it. It must have taken an immense will to do such a thing, but then, will is something all super villains have plenty of.

. . .

It was only April, but it felt like the end of the longest summer of Robbi's life. She had already said goodbye to Dale, who gave her a brotherly hug and said, "I don't know where I'm going, but I'll keep in touch," and to Cara, who accepted her apology with a half-hearted hug.

"Dale was right," Cara had said. "I need some time to get my head together. See if I can get past people thinking I might be a murderer."

"And Guy?" Robbi asked.

Cara shrugged and climbed into her little Suburu. "I guess we'll see. He knows my number."

Old Reliable was packed and ready, but Robbi was procrastinating. She didn't really want to go. As if reading her mind, Mal said, "It's just until you finish up your dissertation. And five hours isn't all that far. I can come and visit, if I can bring Tuck and Miss Scarlett."

"You'd better. I miss them both already. Especially Tuck." She loved Scarlett, of course. How could she not love the dog who had kept Mal from drowning? But Tuck adored Robbi, and the feeling was mutual.

Mal put his hands on her waist and turned her to face him. "I miss *you* already."

They avoided talking about Elinore. She was currently receiving treatment at a psychiatric hospital, near enough for Mal to visit, far enough away that he wouldn't feel obliged to visit every day. "She's still my sister," he'd said, and even though Robbi felt more than a little uncomfortable with a potential sister-in-law who was a criminal mastermind, she loved him for it.

Robbi was loading Falcor's cooler into the back of Old Reliable when Joanne and Miller strolled up, holding hands.

They were a strange and mismatched couple, but their differences somehow complemented each other. In the short time they'd been dating, Joanne had blossomed, and Miller had grown almost bold.

Joanne scooped Robbi up in a bear hug and spun her around. "We made it! Got the last donation ten minutes ago."

"The whole thing?"

Miller grinned. "We just made the transfer—enough to pay Guy's debt in full and b...buy out Hammond's shares, plus Dale's and Cara's, with a little l...left in the faire's coffers until it's needed."

Joanne nodded. "So, whatever they decide about Guy's case, at least we know he's not going to be wearing concrete overshoes."

Mal, watching on the sidelines, piped in. "Unless he gets himself in trouble again."

Robbi didn't think he would. Not the same kind of trouble anyway. His contrition had seemed genuine. "What do you think they'll do to him?"

Joanne winked. "Depends how many women are on the jury. Seriously, though, I think they'll buy his story about Laura, but the coverup will hurt him. Maybe not as bad as it will hurt Hammond, but some."

Robbi wasn't sure about that. Hammond was well known in Sherwood. And when he hobbled onto the witness stand with the help of his cane, at least a few of the jury members were bound to feel some sympathy.

"It's the c...coverup that gets 'em," Miller agreed, and added, "Then again, Guy did call the cops. A crooked cop, but still. It m...might count for something."

"Maybe," Robbi said. "But then what?"

She thought he'd serve a year, maybe two, or maybe weeks, if the jury fell for his roguish charm. But with no shares of his own, he had no claim to the faire, unless the remaining Rennies agreed to give him one. They weren't sure they would. Forgiveness, if it came, would have to be earned. In the meantime, they'd renamed his castle: Bainbridge Castle, after Laura.

Robbi thought her friend would like that.

The morning Tammy is supposed to pick me up, I go to visit Tuck. He's in his pen, which comes as a surprise, but the latch is broken and the gate is open, so I suppose it's not so far from the norm as one might think. He's nosing a plastic ball up a ramp and watching it come down a tube, a simple contraption Elinore made for him before all this trouble began. I know he's missing her. In spite of her crimes, she was always good to him.

He perks up when he sees me, even though he knows this is goodbye. He makes a few pig jokes, which, naturally, lack sophistication, and I tell him a few cat jokes, which he doesn't understand.

I tell him he'd make a good Watson.

Then I go to the parking lot to wait for Tammy. Mal and Robbi wait with me. I sit on Robbi's lap and purr for her, and she rubs my ears. Goodbyes are hard, but as all animals know, they're an important part of life. Robbi has been a good friend, but she isn't my person. Maybe she and Mal will get a kitten.

A familiar car pulls into the lot and parks. I'm already running. Tammy, my Tammy, opens the door, and I leap inside.

Trouble, the famous black cat detective, is finally going home.

ACKNOWLEDGMENTS

My heartfelt thanks to everyone who helped make this book a reality, especially my husband, Mike Hicks, for his eternal support and his engineering expertise; the real Robbie Bryan for lending his name to my heroine; Carolyn Haynes for inviting me on this great adventure; Jean Rabe for sharing her knowledge of law enforcement; Janet Deaver-Pack for her insights into the world of Renaissance Faires; and Tom Luck for his advice about the legalities of the faire shares. I'd also like to thank Michelle Honick, Jalana Hughes, Lynette Ingram, Pamela Schweglar, and Kay Tyler for their valuable input and encouragement; my brother, David Terrell, for the adventure that inspired Tuck; and Mom for being Mom. Thanks, too, to all the family and friends who have been there to offer support and encouragement. I treasure you all.

ABOUT THE AUTHOR

Jaden Terrell is a Shamus Award finalist and the internationally published author of the Nashville-based Jared McKean series. She is a contributor to the *Killer Nashville Noir* anthology, International Thriller Writers' *The Big Thrill* magazine, and *Now Write! Mysteries*, a collection of writing exercises published by Tarcher/Penguin for writers of crime fiction. A recipient of the 2017 Killer Nashville Builder Award, as well as the 2009 Magnolia Award and the 2017 Silver Quill Award for service to the Southeast Chapter of Mystery Writers of America, Terrell offers live and online workshops, coaching, and courses for writers. You can join Jaden's Inner Circle for more news and a free gift.

www.jadenterrell.com

facebook.com/JadenTerrellAuthor

twitter.com/JadenTerrell

instagram.com/jadenterrellauthor

goodreads.com/JadenTerrell

amazon.com/author/jadenterrell

bookbub.com/authors/jaden-terrell

pinterest.com/JadenTerrellAuthor

JOIN JADEN'S INNER CIRCLE

Want to get updates, tidbits, and the occasional contest or freebie? Join my Inner Circle, and you'll also receive a free anthology with short stories from eight different mystery writers, ranging from cozy to hardboiled.

jadenterrell.com/innercircle

ALSO BY JADEN TERRELL

THE JARED MCKEAN PRIVATE DETECTIVE SERIES

Racing the Devil

A Cup Full of Midnight

River of Glass

A Taste of Blood and Ashes

TROUBLE'S DOUBLE CONTEST WINNER

Gus

This is Gustavo, but most people call him "Gus." Those who know him best call him "Gussles Muscles" because he is so sleek and strong! Nobody can deny that Gus is super cool and super powerful now, but that wasn't always the case.

Gus was born in central Florida, and for the first few weeks of his life he roamed the streets of Orlando. He was just a scared little kitten trying to make it in a town that was best known for its mouse. ...But Gus had a plan. He knew that if he learned how to strut around like a tiny little panther, and if he perfected his orchestral collection of bleeps, meeps, purrs, and meows, that the right hoomans would find him and give him his furrever home....which he would then rule with an iron paw for all of eternity! Gus' plan worked like a charm!

Within a few weeks Gus was on his way to his new home with his hooman mom and dad; it was love at first sight. Gus wasted no time in exploring his new abode. He jumped on all the counters (overriding dad's earlier declaration that he would not be allowed on them), zoomed up and down the stairs at lightning speed, and climbed on everything he could find.

On his second day in the house, Gus' mom came home to find him dangling from the blinds by his back leg. Gus' mom and dad were really scared that he had seriously hurt himself, but he made a full recovery. Ever since that day he's had a little strip of white fur on his paw where it got caught.

Gus' hoomans refer to it as his "racing stripe," and it serves as a constant reminder of what a rascal Gus can be! Gus is five years old now, and he can still be a speedy little trouble maker, but most of the time he is sweet, loving, and cuddly.

One of his favorite activities is puzzle time with mom. He likes it so much, in fact, that his go-to move is to sit on the puzzle so that mom can't finish it! It may seem like a ridiculous claim to suggest that Gus is the most amazing and powerful cat in all the land, but in this case, it is quite true. It is an honor and a privilege to be one of Gus' subjects, and we serve him joyfully. We love you, Gus.

— HEATHER PAROLA

FAMILIAR LEGACY

For more contests and news, please join our Familiar Legacy Fan Page on Facebook: www.facebook.com/FamiliarLegacy

Familiar Trouble | Carolyn Haines

Trouble in Dixie | Rebecca Barrett

Trouble in Tallahassee | Claire Matturro

Trouble in Summer Valley | Susan Y. Tanner

Small Town Trouble | Laura Benedict

Trouble in Paradise | Rebecca Barrett

Turning for Trouble | Susan Y. Tanner

Trouble's Wedding Caper | Jen Talty

Bone-a-fied Trouble | Carolyn Haines

Trouble in Action | Susan Y. Tanner

Trouble Most Faire | Jaden Terrell

Made in the USA
Columbia, SC
30 December 2019

85898570R00150